THE ITALIAN'S
PREGNANT
PRISONER

THE ITALIAN'S PREGNANT PRISONER

BY

MAISEY YATES

MILLS & BOON

First published in Great Britain 2017
by Mills & Boon, an imprint of HarperCollins*Publishers*
1 London Bridge Street, London, SE1 9GF

Large Print edition 2018

© 2017 Maisey Yates

ISBN: 978-0-263-07332-4

MIX
Paper from
responsible sources
FSC™ C007454

This book is produced from independently certified FSC™ paper to ensure responsible forest management. For more information visit www.harpercollins.co.uk/green.

Printed and bound in Great Britain
by CPI Group (UK) Ltd, Croydon, CR0 4YY

To the Presents team.

You believed in me first.

I didn't know when I sent in my chapters
eight years ago that this was where it would lead.

I'm so glad it did.

CHAPTER ONE

Once upon a time...

LET DOWN YOUR HAIR...

Charlotte Adair's heart was pounding so hard she was sure the person next to her could hear it. And she was shaking. Shaking and fighting against the rising tide of emotions and memories that were threatening to compromise her ability to think straight.

Although, it could easily be argued that her being here at all was proving she lacked any ability to think with clarity.

She had escaped. For five years she had been free.

But there was unfinished business. *Rafe.*

He would always be unfinished business. There would be no fixing that. But she could *see* him. She could see him one more time.

And, at least, he wouldn't be able to see her.

Pain burst in her chest, hot and acidic, her stomach tightening. Yes, his abandonment had hurt her. Immeasurably. But that didn't mean the thought of such a powerful man being injured in the way he had been wasn't painful.

Of course, any thoughts of Rafe were painful.

And as she stood in the darkened corner of the antechamber that led into the ballroom, her palms beginning to sweat, the red gown she was wearing started to feel so tight she could scarcely breathe.

She couldn't hold off the memories any longer…

"Let down your hair."

"You know I'm not allowed to," Charlotte said, moving away from Rafe, every nerve ending in her body tingling. Every part of her demanding that she follow his simply issued command, regardless of the consequences.

Which was basically the same demand she'd

been issuing to herself from the moment she'd first seen him.

She wanted him. Whatever that had meant at first, she hadn't fully known. Only that she wanted to be near him. Always.

"I see. And what exactly are the rules concerning men in your bedroom?"

She blushed, her skin heating all over. "Well, I would assume that it's frowned upon. Of course, it is nothing my father ever thought to forbid me expressly from. I suppose I'm meant to take it as read."

Rafe smiled, and she felt the impact of it all the way down to her toes. He was the most beautiful man she had ever seen. That had been her very first thought about seeing him when he'd come to work for her father two years earlier.

She wasn't entirely sure of the circumstances, only that he was an apprentice of sorts, which made her stomach tremble in a not-too-pleasant way. Because while the circumstances of her father's business were kept largely secret to her, she wasn't stupid. Yes, she lived a secluded life at his villa in Italy, transplanted from their native United States when Charlotte had been just a child, but in that seclusion she had taken the opportunity to learn how to gain information by quiet observation.

Charlotte had become part of the wallpaper in the villa many years ago, and as a result she was often underestimated. She liked it that way.

Being invisible.

But then Rafe had appeared, and he had not allowed her to remain invisible. He had *seen* her. From the first. She had been sixteen the first time she'd laid eyes on him, when she had been certain that her heart was going to claw its way up her throat and out of her mouth. Not just because he was beautiful—though, he was certainly beautiful. In his early twenties at the time, with broad shoulders, a jaw so square she thought she might cut her finger on it, and dark, fathomless eyes that she wanted desperately to get lost in.

He was a tall man, well over six feet, and she had the feeling that if she were to walk up to him and stand just in front of him that she would only come up to the middle of his chest. Which, she could not help but think, would be solid, strong, perfect to rest against.

Yes, her obsession had begun that first moment, and it had not abated. Apparently, it had been the same for him. He had tried to warn her away from him. But she'd persisted. She'd made a fool of herself, following him around. But it had worked. Eventually, he had stopped telling her to go away. Eventually, they had begun to form a friendship.

Except, she supposed friends didn't have to sneak around. Friends did not have to wait until the house was dark, and everyone was safely asleep to meet out in the stables, or to catch a moment with one another in the brilliant light of day out in one of the fields well away from the house.

It was chaste. Always.

Until one afternoon when they'd been in the corner of the barn, and he had told her it was time for him to go back to his post—whatever that meant—and she'd been filled with a strange kind of desperation that she could not fathom or fight.

She had reached up, touched his face with her fingertips. And then she'd had his iron grip wrapped around her wrist, his dark eyes burning hotter than she had ever seen them before.

Before she could protest—before she could question anything—his mouth had been on hers. Claiming. Marking her as his own.

She had never been kissed before that moment. Hadn't even thought much about it. But kissing Rafe was like touching the surface of the sun. She could hardly bear it.

It was too hot. Too bright. Too much.

And far too brief.

But that night, he had climbed the trellis and come into her room. Her tower bedroom, high above the rest of the house, separated from everyone, as she always was. No one came into her bedroom.

But he had. And he had treated her to another kiss. Then another.

He had come to her room every night for the

past two weeks. Their kisses had gotten longer, deeper. They'd begun shedding clothes. Lying on the bed together. Trading intimacies she would have found shocking before him. Would have found shocking if it were with anyone *but* him.

With Rafe, all these things felt right. She'd been asking him for more. Asking him to take her virginity. But so far he'd kept it to pleasuring her, and never taking things to their ultimate conclusion.

She had been okay to wait. But tonight she felt urgency. Tonight, there was a rock in her stomach, and she knew that she had to tell him about the conversation she'd had with her stepmother earlier that day.

Her father didn't often speak to her, if he did at all. Most of the relevant information was conveyed through Josefina, her stepmother, who was the most hardened, suspicious person Charlotte had ever known.

And given Charlotte lived in a compound with criminals, that was quite a feat.

Earlier today she had informed Charlotte that

her father's ultimate purpose for her was about to be fulfilled. He had found another kingpin in a corner of Italy Charlotte had never been to who was looking for a wife. And it was an alliance her father wanted to cement with his own bloodline. A dynastic union. The one use he could think of for a daughter he had never wanted.

Josefina seemed nothing but happy to be rid of the stepdaughter she had always seemed jealous of. A jealousy Charlotte could not understand, given she was a glorified prisoner in her father's home. But Josefina had once been a poor girl from the village her father's estate was built near, and she had clawed her way from poverty to being Michael Adair's mistress, then ultimately his wife. She wasn't quiet about that achievement, and it was Charlotte's belief that her stepmother was secretly afraid she might someday lose her elevated position, which made her a bit vicious.

She had certainly seemed vicious when telling Charlotte of her upcoming marital fate.

Dimly, Charlotte had always thought that her life might come to this. Because her father was nothing if not a medieval lord, the master of his keep and all who depended on him for anything. And of course it was not outside the realm of imagination that he would try to cement his power in the criminal world through marriages. Like a dark king, trading family members to prevent wars. Or to start them. Depending on the present circumstance.

But even though part of her had always known it was a possibility, she had done her very best not to think of it. And now, there was Rafe.

Rafe, who made love and sex something that wasn't theoretical. Rather, something that she wanted. Something that she craved. Not in a general sense. She wanted it with him.

The idea of sharing her body with someone else... It could not be endured. Her need for Rafe, for his touch, his kiss, for everything... It was so intimate. It went deeper than the electric need that sparked over her skin.

It was heart. *He* was her heart.

"Yes," he said, "I suppose that is the letter of the law, if not the spirit of it." His dark eyes turned intense, a black flame that burned through her. "I would like you to break some rules for me. I know your hair is considered quite the asset. You're not allowed to cut it—is that true?"

Charlotte touched her heavy bun. "Not entirely. I get the ends trimmed. But yes. My father considers my hair to be part of my beauty." And the importance of her beauty had become shockingly clear with her marriage deal being brokered.

"Creepy."

She forced out a laugh. "You work for him. And here you are."

"I only work for him until my debt is repaid. I have no loyalty to your father. On that you can trust me."

It was the first time Rafe had said anything like this to her. "I didn't…I didn't realize."

"I am forbidden from speaking of it. But then, I am certain that I am also forbidden from being in here. And I'm also forbidden from touching you like this." He put his hand on her cheek, and then he kissed her. "Let down your hair," he whispered against her lips.

This time, she obeyed. For him. Only for him…

* * *

Charlotte was dragged back to the present, and her heart was beating out of control, as it had been in the memory. It had only been a couple of weeks after that when everything had fallen apart. When she had been left devastated, wounded beyond the healing of that devastation.

When Josefina had told her that Rafe had gone, that he didn't want her. And that she had no choice but to go and marry Stefan. Charlotte had protested. So much so, that she had found herself locked up. So much so that she had seen the true nature of her father. He did not love her. Not at all. He would kill her if she didn't marry the man of his choosing; that was what he'd told her. And Charlotte had been ready to believe it.

She had also not been ready to accept her fate. Because if there was one thing that being with Rafe had taught her, it was that there was more to life than the villa. More to life than her tower bedroom. More to intimacy with a man than a simple transaction.

And she had wanted those things. All of them.

So when her father had paid his men to transport her across the country and they had stopped at a petrol station in the middle of nowhere she had taken her chance.

She'd slipped from her restraints and fled, running deep into the woods, certain they wouldn't follow her there. Somehow, she was right. They had searched for her along the highways, perhaps checking in with passing motorists and various business owners.

They certainly hadn't expected *her*—cosseted princess of the Adair family empire—to take her chances with the wolves and foxes out in the thick forest.

But she had.

Ultimately, had found a certain measure of safety living in rural Germany, moving from cottage to cottage, never settling in one place too long, taking simple positions at shops and farms over the years.

It had been a lonely existence, but in many ways freeing.

It wasn't until years later that she had seen

anything of Rafe again. But then, there he was, splashed across the cover of a newspaper. The story of a man who had worked his way up from nothing, from the Italian slums, to become one of the wealthiest men on earth.

A blind man. Wounded in an accident that he refused to speak of.

After that, she saw him on the covers of papers quite a lot. It never got easier. It never got less painful. She ached for him. For what they might have had, had he truly loved her as she had believed he had. For the accident that had taken his sight.

She thought very little about his billions. If only because she had never truly doubted that Rafe would overcome his circumstances in a spectacular way. He was a singular man. He always had been. No one compared to him. And no one ever would.

It was why, when she had gotten the news of her father's death, when she had found out about the invitation under his name to this event, and the fact that Rafe would also be in attendance, that she had decided to take her chances.

With her father out of the picture, no one was coming for her. And she very much doubted any of his men would recognize her now. She was no longer an eighteen-year-old girl.

And as for Rafe... Well, he would never see her. Just as he would never see anything ever again.

But she could see him. She needed to do that. Needed to put that part of her life behind her completely so she could move on. Her time of seclusion was at an end. And he was wrapped all up in it.

She was done hiding. But she had some ghosts to vanquish.

She took a fortifying breath and moved out of the shadows and into the light. She could honestly say it was the first time in five years she had done this. For the first time in five years, she wasn't hiding.

She sensed that heads were turning, following her progress as she made her way through the ballroom. But she didn't care. She wasn't here for generic admiration. Or curiosity. She was here for him.

She had dressed up for him. Even if it was foolish. For one thing, he wouldn't be able to see her. For another, she didn't want him to.

It didn't take her long to see him, though. Her eyes were drawn to him, like a magnet. He was near the center of the ballroom, standing and making conversation with a group of men in suits. He was the tallest. The handsomest. He had always been the singularly most beautiful man she had ever seen. And he still was. Except at thirty he was much more mature than he'd been at twenty-five. He had filled out, his chest thicker, his face more chiseled. Dark stubble sat heavy on his jaw, and she wondered…she wondered what it would be like to touch his face with it there.

She hadn't touched a man since Rafe. She'd had no interest.

She needed to find some interest. Because she was going to have a normal life. After she claimed the inheritance she knew that she still had—untouched—in a trust at the bank in London, she was going to start her life in earnest.

Maybe go to school. Maybe start a shop of her own, since she had always enjoyed working in them over the past few years. Had enjoyed not being lonely.

Whatever she did, it would be her choice. And that was the point.

She didn't know what answers she had expected to find here. Right now, the only clear answer seemed to be that her body, her heart, was still affected by him.

He excused himself from the group, and suddenly, he was walking her way. And she froze. Like a deer caught in the headlights. Or rather, like a woman staring at Rafe Costa.

She certainly wasn't the only woman staring. He moved with fluid grace, and if she didn't know better, she would never have known his sight was impaired at all.

He was coming closer, and as he did her heart

tripped over itself, her hands beginning to shake. She wished she could touch him.

Oh, she wanted it more than anything. In that moment, she wanted it more than her next breath. To put her hands on Rafe Costa's face one more time. To kiss those lips again. To place her hand over his chest and see if she could still make his heart race.

It was easy to forget that her stepmother had told her how Rafe had left, taking an incentive offered by her father to end his tenure there earlier. How he had thought nothing of Charlotte when he left. Nothing of all the promises he had made to her.

Yes, it was so easy to forget all of that. It was easy to forget that and remember instead the way it had felt when he had kissed her. Touched her. The way that she had begged him to use more than his hands between her thighs, more than his mouth. The way she had pleaded with him to take her virginity, to make her his in every way.

But he hadn't.

For honor, he had said. And for her protection.

Except, really, he had never wanted her. At least, not enough to risk anything. So he had simply been toying with her.

She should remember that. Her treacherous, traitorous body should remember that well. But it didn't. Instead, it was fluttering. As if a host of butterflies had been set loose inside her.

He came closer, closer still, passing through the crowd of people, everyone moving out of the way for him, as though he was Moses parting the sea.

Time seemed to slow. Everything around her. Her heartbeat. Her breathing.

Suddenly, he was there. So close that if she wanted to she could reach out and touch the edge of his sleeve with her fingertips.

Could bump into him accidentally, just to make contact. He wouldn't know it was her. He couldn't.

Suddenly, he turned. He was looking past her, his dark eyes unseeing, unfocused. But then, he reached out and unerringly grabbed hold of her wrist, dragging her toward his muscular body.

"Charlotte."

CHAPTER TWO

IT WAS IMPOSSIBLE.

Charlotte—for all intents and purposes—had disappeared five years ago. She hadn't simply disappeared; she had gone off to marry another man.

The triumphant smile on her stepmother's face was the last thing he had seen. The last thing he had ever seen. Beyond gray, amorphous shapes.

He mostly hung close to the walls in situations like this. He had a cane to help him navigate, but in a crowd this thick it was still difficult. Though, in a crowd this thick it was also normal to run into people. So there was that.

He could see sharp contrasts between light and darkness, but he couldn't make out features or colors. Nothing subtle.

But when he had walked by her, he had caught

her scent. And in that moment, he had seen so many things. Color and light bursting through his mind, vivid and sharp. Sun-drenched days in Tuscany, that had been hell on earth except for her. Soft, pearlescent skin that was too fine, too exquisite for him to touch. And yet he had. And that beautiful blond hair that her father had had a strange obsession with.

Glossy, impossibly long and always kept wound up in a bun so that no one could truly see it or appreciate it. Memory gripped him tight...

"Let down your hair," he rasped against her throat as he kissed her, lying down on her large four-poster bed.

He begged her for that privilege, every night. The privilege of running his hands through her hair. Touching the silken strands, seeing her naked, her hair cascading over her pale body like a waterfall, light pink nipples just barely visible through the golden curtain.

She reached up, taking the pins out, obeying his command. In the past weeks since he had begun coming into her room he had asked her to do this for him every night, and every night she had complied. The fact that she never took it down before he appeared led him to believe that she enjoyed this game. Of his commands, and her acquiescence.

It was fine with him. He liked it too.

It was dangerous. This game. Easy to pretend that it was some sort of harmless assignation. That they might get caught, and might suffer a severe scolding. But Rafe was under no illusions. If he were caught with Charlotte, her father would have him killed. If Charlotte were found not a virgin, after her father had taken great pains to seclude her away from the rest of the world, Rafe would be killed. And possibly Charlotte, as well.

And so, he didn't take her virginity. Rather, he pushed the boundaries every night. And every night she begged him for more. Every night, he declined. But he was becoming weak. He would not be able to hold out for much longer. And in truth, he didn't intend to.

He simply needed to get to a place where he

had shored up the assets he needed to be free of her father. He could hardly plunge Charlotte into a life of poverty after she had lived the cosseted existence of a gentleman gangster's daughter. Michael Adair's empire had the semblance of legitimacy, but it was anything but.

To most of the world he appeared to be a businessman. But that was only because the world didn't look too closely. Not at fabulously wealthy, powerful men who could offer a great many favors, and do untold amounts of damage if they were crossed. It benefited no one to examine those things too deeply. And so nobody did.

Rafe knew all too well about the power men like Michael wielded. He knew too what it was to go from a spoiled, cushioned life to one of abject poverty. His father was not unlike Michael Adair. Oh, he might not be a criminal, but he thought nothing of using the people in his life until they were spent.

Until he had no more use for them but to grind them under his boot for fun. That was what Rafe remembered most about the father he hadn't seen since he was five years old. How much he seemed to relish causing pain.

When he had kicked Rafe and his mother out onto the streets, the man had seemed to enjoy their distress. Or, if not that, then the fact he had the power to do so.

Power. Yes, men like that loved power.

And Rafe had spent many years with no power at all. Begging. Stealing. Doing whatever he could to help his mother survive.

He had begun doing odd petty crimes with a group of boys. Delivering packages that he never asked about the contents of. Things like that.

He'd ended up getting caught by the police and charged with running drugs, in spite of the fact that he was only a boy. And a boy who'd had no idea what he was handling at that.

It was through that arrest that he'd met Michael Adair.

It was only much later that Rafe had realized the man must have had a connection to the drugs. To the particular ring of petty criminals Rafe had been working with.

Michael Adair had not only given Rafe his freedom; he had also provided Rafe with an education, paying for him to attend one of the finest private schools in Europe. Rafe had accepted greedily. Uncaring of what it might mean in the future.

Michael had promised him someday he would collect the favor. And indeed, he had made good on that threat.

For years, he had done various errands for Michael in Rome. Until finally, he had been brought to the estate to apprentice under the man himself.

That was when he'd really gotten to know the man he'd aligned himself with. Had seen how hard he was. How entirely without morals.

Rafe had asked him once why he had shown such an interest in a young boy from the streets. Why he'd helped him at all, much less sent him to school and provided for him.

He'd said it was because he didn't have a son. And he had thought perhaps Rafe was the protégé he needed.

Rafe might have been shocked or upset if he

weren't already the son of an amoral bastard. As it was, he just figured he might as well take advantage. At least this particular amoral bastard wanted to give him a hand up, unlike his actual father.

But after school he had started getting a deeper look at Michael Adair's twisted empire. By then he was living at the estate and there was no leaving. Not without being killed.

The entire business made Rafe ill. Michael was ruthless. He didn't care who was hurt by his business practices. And he was not above intimidation, or even murder to get what he wanted. He had a host of enforcers who meted out punishments on those who did not comply with his wishes. And Rafe could only count himself fortunate that he had not been forced to be part of that side of the business.

No, he was being taught the business. Because Michael had no son. And he wanted Rafe to be able to take control of the business portion, the front of house part of the empire.

But that did not mean that he found Rafe to

be good enough for his daughter, and Rafe was under no illusions that it would be the case. Rafe had also decided that while he was content to get any education he could get from Michael, he was certainly never going to overtake the man's evil empire.

No. He was going to escape at his first opportunity. And he was going to do it with Charlotte.

Then. Then he would make her his.

She shook her head, her hair falling around her in a silken wave. His stomach tightened. And he couldn't breathe. He'd had more women than he could count. A side effect of being a young boy unsupervised far too early. One who looked much older than he was the moment adolescence had hit.

But none had ever affected him like this. None had ever made him feel as though his heart were being pulled out of his chest through his mouth. Had ever made him feel like he might die if he didn't touch her. But also made him feel so protective that…he would rather cut off his own hands than do her harm. And it was that need, that need that overrode all else, that gave him the strength to resist her, night after night.

He leaned in, sliding his fingers through her hair, lifting the silken strands to his face, and inhaling deeply.

Roses. Lavender. And something he couldn't name. Something that belonged only to her...

Rafe dragged himself back to the present. And to the feel of the woman he was currently holding on to. Soft. She was so soft. It had to be Charlotte. It could only be her.

Of course, it had been five years since he had touched a woman, so perhaps, his memory was faulty. Perhaps, they were all this soft. But he didn't think so.

Michael Adair was dead. And he had been on Rafe's mind this morning. Perhaps, that was why his body was playing tricks on him now.

Or perhaps, it was why Charlotte had resurfaced.

"Come with me," he said, his voice hard.

He held on to her with one arm, casually sweeping the ground in front of them with his cane in his other hand.

She said nothing. Didn't protest. Didn't speak at all. Frustration bubbled up inside him. And he wished...oh, how he wished he could see her face. Yes, his other senses had been honed quite a bit since the accident. But in this moment, though, senses could not replace his sight. Not by a long shot.

He took them out of the ballroom, into some kind of alcove. Perhaps no one was around, it didn't seem as though anyone was. But if they were, he doubted they would have the balls to interrupt them. Something else Rafe had honed over the past five years was a fearsome reputation. He was a man who took no prisoners. He acted ethically. He was bound and determined that he would. That he would never bear any resemblance to Michael Adair, or to any man like him. But he was also determined that he would never go back to the streets he had come from.

It was power that insulated a man. He knew that well. The only reason he had been at Michael's mercy in the first place was because he had been vulnerable. Because he lacked resources. Because he lacked power.

He had made a vow that he would never return to that place. Never. There was no longer any vulnerability inside of him. And truly, his blindness—nature's last gasp at ensuring he wasn't all powerful—had only spurred him on to work harder.

It was an accident he wished hadn't happened. He didn't want to give it too much credit in his life. However, he was also certain enough that it had made him work harder. That it made him yet more determined to appear capable, infallible.

He was also certain that early on it had caused a great many to underestimate him. So when his corporation gobbled up theirs, when his success put them out of business—his electronics manufacturing conglomerate slowly and steadily taking over the world—they simply hadn't seen it coming.

Something he found deliciously ironic.

"What the hell are you doing here?" he asked.

"Has your husband set you free? Or has he simply let you out for the night?"

"I...I..."

Was it her? Was that her voice? It had been so long. And memory was not infallible. If this was simply something conjured up out of his darkest desires, out of need he should no longer feel, his rage with himself would know no bounds.

"Charlotte Adair." He said her name like a curse. "Is that your last name anymore? After marrying Stefan did you take his last name?"

"I think you must be mistaken," she said, her voice a low whisper.

He slid his hand up her arm, following the line to her collarbone, up the side of her neck and to her chin, where he gripped her between his thumb and forefinger. "I am never mistaken. You would do well to remember that." He leaned in, and he could smell her again. Lavender. Roses. *Charlotte.*

His heart beat her name over and over again.

It had to be her. No woman had affected him

like this in the past five years. No woman had affected him at all.

And then he'd walked through that ballroom and caught her scent, touched her skin. It was like being born again.

"If you lie to me, I will make you pay. There will be no end to what it will cost you."

She began to tremble beneath his touch, and he slid his thumb upward, along her lower lip, heat and arousal tightening his gut.

"You cannot lie to me," he whispered, his mouth now so close to hers he could feel her breath. "You might have a husband, but believe me, there is no man on earth who knows you as well as I do."

She was burned into his memory in a way no one else could be. Because losing his head over Charlotte had nearly cost him everything. Had been a turning point in his life. He could not walk away from it, not really. He bore the mark of it.

Not just his vision, but the ugly scars on his body from where he had fallen off the balcony.

From where he had been pushed.

"My…my father is dead," she said, the words rushed. "I've come to London to sort out some of his business."

He laughed, the sound cold and hard even to his own ears. "Silly girl. Did you think for one moment that I would be unaware of your father's death? I nearly gave my staff a holiday. In celebration."

He slid his hand down her throat, holding it gently, feeling the flutter of her pulse beneath his thumb.

"I was under no illusion you would have given them a holiday so that you could wallow in your grief," she said, her breathing quick and shallow, betraying her fear when her tone of voice did not.

"I opened my best bottle of champagne that night."

She shifted, and he had a feeling she was looking directly at him now. Looking him full in the face, when before she had not been. "So did I. Do not think you have a monopoly on despising that man."

"Probably the last remaining thing we have in common, *cara mia.*" She stiffened beneath his touch.

"It would not surprise me."

Her pulse was racing beneath his thumb, and he knew that his own heart was pounding just as hard. He was angry with her. So angry. He wanted to destroy her. Destroy her in the way he had been destroyed by the loss of her. By her betrayal.

But he also wanted her. That protection he had extended to her, the virginity he had preserved, simply so that she could throw it away to another man, so that she could marry another, galled him.

It had been his by rights. And out of some misguided sense of chivalry that he no longer possessed he had not laid claim to it.

"Is your husband here?" he asked.

She hesitated. "No."

"I believe you and I have unfinished business." He changed the way he held her, yet again moving his thumb up to her mouth, to trace her plush lips. "Do you not agree?"

He heard a faint sniff, and he imagined her tossing her head back, her expression haughty. He had seen her do it many times before. Years ago. "I don't know what you're talking about."

"Charming. But I think you do." He moved his fingertips to the edge of her mouth, then back down the side of her neck, coming to rest on her pulse. "This feels just as I remember it. I make your blood run faster. This makes me wonder if I still make you wet."

She gasped, and he waited for a slap across the face that didn't come.

"I'm frightened," she said, her voice breathy.

"I don't believe that. A woman who would dare set foot in London, into a place where you had to know I would be, so soon after her father's death... Well, I don't believe she's afraid of anything. No. I do not believe this is fear, Charlotte."

"What you believe or don't believe doesn't automatically become truth."

He chuckled. "See, that simply isn't true. I'm richer than your father ever was. People do my bidding, not because they fear me but because of what I can do for them. What I wish often becomes truth easily enough."

Five years. Five years since he had touched a woman. Longer since he'd had sex with one. There had been no one else from the moment he'd met her. And he'd held back out of deference to her innocence.

Now it had been five years since he had touched her.

"I can make you want me," he said.

And he hated that, for the first time in years, he doubted himself. Because as certain as he was of a great many things, he could not be certain that she would want a scarred, blind man in her bed.

"What exactly are you proposing?" she asked, her words cool.

"I'll make it very clear. I don't care what you've been doing for the past five years. I don't care that you married Stefan. I don't care what you do tomorrow, for that matter. I care about tonight. Tonight, I want to make sure we finish what is between us. Tonight. I want you in my bed."

He jerked back when trembling fingers touched

his lower lip. The shock of it immobilized him. It had been so long since he had been touched. So he stood, absolutely still as she traced his lower lip, his upper lip, mimicking what he had just done for her. She traced his jaw, and then moved her fingers featherlight down the side of his neck, where they came to rest on his pulse.

"Unless you're afraid of me," she said, "then it appears I still have the same effect on you that I once did."

He held her chin, keeping her still. "That may be. But one thing has changed. I do not love you, Charlotte. Quite the opposite. If I take you to my bed, you will be giving yourself to a man who hates you. Though, I wonder if that matters? Because it certainly doesn't matter to me. I find that I want you regardless."

"One night?" And this time, a slight tremble worked its way into her words.

"Just one," he responded.

She let out a long, slow breath that echoed in the corridor around them. "Okay. One night."

CHAPTER THREE

CHARLOTTE WAS CRAZY. She supposed that was what years in isolation would do to a person. Not that she had ever been isolated truly. She had made friends wherever she had gone, but it was always on the internal understanding that she wouldn't be in one place for long. And, of course, she had been unable to share the truth behind her circumstances, no matter how wonderful her new friends had seemed.

It was too dangerous for them. Too dangerous for her.

That always put distance between herself and her friends, no matter how much she wished it wasn't there.

But her old life—no matter how far she ran from it—always had claws in her. She had spent five years looking over her shoulder. Five years fearing that one day her father's men, or Stefan's, would show up at the door of her home, or one of the shops that she worked in. Five years living abroad, traveling from place to place. Hiding.

But now her father was dead. And the last remaining claw stuck deep into her flesh was Rafe. Yes, she had come to London tonight to catch one last glimpse of him before moving on. But perhaps, this was better. Perhaps, this was what she needed.

She had been prepared to give him her virginity five years ago. He was the man she had meant for it. Perhaps, it was fate. No matter what the ensuing years had brought.

Yes, Rafe had hurt her. His abandonment had wounded her deeply. But, in the end, there would have been nothing he could have done for her. And she could not have gone back to him while her father lived.

If her father had known where she was, he would have come for her. And he certainly would have killed Rafe.

Her fantasies of him had been wound around

anger, grief and sadness for the past five years. And, yes, she had blamed him for some things. In the dark of the night, when she lay there, feeling like there was a heavy weight resting on her chest, she had internally raged at him for not saving her. For not climbing the tower and carrying her away with him. Off to live in a forest somewhere. Where mice and birds would build them…a house or something.

Not a care. No contact with the outside.

But this was the real world. It wasn't a fairy tale, and she knew that none of that was actually possible.

It made for a lovely fantasy. But in the end, she'd had to escape the tower on her own. In the end, it had been up to her to save herself. Bringing anyone with her would have only put them in danger.

So, it didn't matter that Rafe had left. It was better. Better for him.

And she still hurt when she thought of him.

So maybe this was what she needed to do.

Maybe this was the grand letting go that she required. Maybe. Just maybe.

Whether this was the road to salvation or perdition, she imagined it remained to be seen. Either way, she was on it.

In his limousine.

It had been a great many years since she had traveled this way. Even tonight, dressed in a gown that had cost her entire savings, she had taken a cab.

She hadn't worried much about her savings, because she would come into her money in the next week or so. And tonight was supposed to be a strange fantasy. Or really, the last chapter on a life she had never chosen to live in the first place. That she wanted.

She tightened her hold on her clutch purse, staring straight ahead, the city lights flashing in her face as they drove.

Rafe pressed a hand to her shoulder. "Just checking to make sure you were still there."

"I don't believe for a moment that you thought I had gone." As if she was going to silently fling herself out onto the London streets and tuck and roll in her beautiful red gown.

"No," he said. "I can hear you breathing. I can almost hear your heart beating. Tell me, Charlotte. Are you nervous?"

"I told you I was," she said. "I told you I was frightened."

"You are not frightened. You know I won't harm you. I had a great many chances to do that. A great many times when I was alone with you, and I still possessed my sight. When I could have done anything to you, and by the time you had screamed it would've been too late for your father's guards to rescue you. I would say that with your father gone you have absolutely nothing to fear from me. Any leverage that you might have been has long since ceased to be."

What a strange thing. The introduction of the thought that he might have harmed her back then to escape working for her father. Or that he might have threatened to harm her. It had never occurred to her then. Never occurred to her that he might be using her. Because she had been so young. Because she had trusted him implicitly.

But he hadn't harmed her or held her hostage then.

And, in order for him to wish her harm now, it would have to be personal. He would have to want some kind of revenge against her. And for what? He was the one who had left her. And, if it had demonstrated anything it was that his feelings for her had never been all that strong.

His refusal to take her virginity had been all about him hedging his bets and saving his own skin. It had nothing to do with *honoring* her. With *protecting* her, as he had pretended it did all those years ago.

"I don't think you're going to hurt me," she said, her throat tight, speaking nearly impossible. "What would the headline say, after all? It isn't as though people didn't see us leave together. Nobody knows who I am, but if they found my body in a hotel room, they would connect me to you soon enough."

She looked over at him, saw his lip curl upward. He was still touching her. Still maintaining contact. "Please. I'm not going to kill you. That is more your father's style than mine. Such displays hold no interest for me. I have built my empire on the rock. Not the sand."

"Excellent. So when the rains come down your house will stand firm."

"That is the hope," he said, his tone caustic.

It all seemed so absurd suddenly. That she was in this dress, in this limo, with Rafe. She could hardly figure out how she'd gotten there. Just a few hours ago she'd slipped the dress on, ready so sneak quietly into the ball, see him just for a moment and then leave. But he'd...sensed her.

She hadn't counted on that.

She should know that anticipating Rafe was impossible.

"What is it you want with me?" she asked.

"I should think it is quite obvious. I want no more than to claim what I want. What I have always wanted. I want your body, Charlotte. I want all that was kept from me five years ago. Weeks of foreplay only to have my prize stolen from me. I did not take kindly to it then. I don't like it now."

She frowned. "How was I *stolen* from you? You left."

"I left? Is that the story then?" He chuckled, hard and dark. "I was certainly shown the way out."

"I was told one morning that you had gone, and that I would be sent to marry Stefan. That my father knew about our relationship and that he had offered you a bargain to leave. And that you chose the money he gave you over me. That you chose your freedom. I was hurt, Rafe, but I could understand. I know how my father is. I know what a wonderful thing it would be to be free of him. If I could've been free of him so easily, I would have done so. I'm not going to say I wasn't angry. But I accepted it."

She looked over at him, his face illuminated as they passed a lit-up storefront. His expression was blank.

"I did not leave you," he said finally.

"You didn't?"

"No. I was…told that you left. I was told you had gone to marry the man of your father's choosing. The path of least resistance."

She laughed. But there was no humor in it. "I suppose the fact that either of us believed anything relayed to us by Josefina or my father makes us fools. They were master manipulators, always. And that wasn't even a very master manipulation. It was just two vulnerable people ready to believe the worst, I suppose. Ready to believe the worst of the world and all of the people in it."

"Why would you ever believe anything else?"

Silence stretched between them.

"I do want this," she said, curling her hands into fists. "Do you?"

The streetlight caught his exquisite face, highlighting his razor-sharp cheekbones, the curve of his lips. Her heart stuttered.

"I have wanted little else for the past five years. I have amassed a great fortune, Charlotte, and there are two things that I have never been able to obtain in spite of my newfound wealth and power. My sight, and you. You, I can have. You, I will have. Seeing as I cannot have the other."

The car pulled up to a beautiful building, all ornate stonework, well lit, exquisitely visible even in the dark.

"We have arrived," he said. He removed his hand from her shoulder, and the two of them sat in the car and waited. The driver opened the door, and Rafe got out, his hand resting on the car as he walked around to the curbside, his cane sweeping the ground.

Her heart folded up like it was made of paper. Fragile and easily torn. Of all the misunderstandings between them, this was not one of them. Rafe had lost his sight, and though she had known it for a while now, it still hurt her. It wounded her that he was hurt. That he had lost something of himself.

And the fact that her father and stepmother had lied to them both...

Yes, she and Rafe did deserve this night. Whatever else lay ahead, they deserved this.

Her door opened, and she looked out to see

Rafe, extending his hand to her. She hesitated, but only for a moment. And then she curled her fingers around his, and he lifted her from the limousine. She landed against his chest, her palm spread over his muscles, her hand over his beating heart.

It was raging. Just as hard as her own.

"Rafe…"

"We must go inside," he said. "Now. Otherwise, I'm likely to take you up against the side of the building."

For a moment, Charlotte couldn't quite work out why that would be a bad thing. "Okay," she said, her voice thick.

With a firm hand, Rafe led her into the building, and the two of them walked across the small gilded space to an elevator with golden doors. They swung open, and she followed him in, having to take two steps to his one.

Clearly, this was his domain. There was no hesitation in any of his movements. The only indication that he wasn't able to visualize his surroundings in the quick sweep of his cane across the floor.

Suddenly, her breath was coming harder, faster. She hadn't seen this man in five years. It had taken two weeks of physical intimacy to build up five years' worth of fantasies. And now she was here. Now she was here, but he wasn't *her* Rafe anymore. Wasn't a man in indentured servitude to her father, but one of the most powerful businessmen in the world. A man with billions of dollars. A man newspapers wrote of in hyperbolic phrasing. A man that women spoke of with awed reverence.

That thought sent a kick straight to her gut. She wondered how many women he'd been with since their time in her tower. How many women he'd touched. Kissed. Been inside.

Of course, she had never truly had him. So it seemed silly to worry about who else might have.

Well, you'll have him tonight. And those other women won't matter. This isn't about them. This is about you. It's for you. It's not for anyone else.

Yes, she had been stagnant for so long, and she was done with it.

Tonight, she would have Rafe, and she wouldn't concern herself with the consequences.

Before she was prepared, the lift reached its destination and the doors slid open. They were here.

They hadn't even kissed. In five years, they hadn't kissed. She had said yes to this because of a mere touch. Because of his firm, warm hold on her throat.

She couldn't go back now. She wasn't even certain that she wanted to.

He took her hand and led her inside, and she followed.

The loft was Spartan. Wide swaths of floor left blank, furniture pushed more or less against the walls.

He took his jacket off and hung it on a peg, and then placed his cane in a holder by the door. He straightened, his focus on the black space before them.

"My circumstances have changed quite a bit," he remarked, gesturing to the space around them.

"Your circumstances never mattered to me." She examined him, the hard set of his jaw, that cold, closed-off expression on his face. Tension radiated from that big, strong body in waves. She wanted to touch him. Wanted to move away from him, as well. He was frightening. Compelling and magnetic. All at the same time.

Finally, he spoke. "My circumstances mattered a great deal to me."

"Of course they did," she whispered. "I didn't mean..."

"I do not want your apologies, Charlotte. This is not an evening for recrimination. Not now. You and I should've both forgotten about a youthful dalliance a long time ago. Clearly, we did not. So, there is business yet to be finished between us. And I, for one, need to see it done."

After that, there was no waiting. He reached out, and she went to him. Then, he wrapped his arm around her waist and drew her up against his hard, muscular body.

He took hold of her chin, as he had done back at the party. Only this time, he didn't stop. This time, there was no slow, careful examination. There was no hesitation at all.

His lips crashed down on hers, unerring, his tongue parting her, delving deep into her mouth, slick and hot, and somehow even more than she had remembered.

He had been her first kiss. Her only kiss.

She had never let a man get so close to her since then. She had known that that way contained only heartbreak, and she had no desire to experience heartbreak again. Not when everything in her life was still in such peril. When it was still dangerous to breathe in too deeply, much less forge any kind of true emotional bond with somebody.

And it had never seemed…it had never seemed right to pursue a purely physical relationship. Perhaps because of the intensity of what she had felt for Rafe. She wasn't sure. Either way, the idea had never really appealed to her.

Except, that was what she was doing now. With

him. There had been no promises made, and she wouldn't ask him for any.

This was about creating a new life. The life that she wanted, on her own terms, and free of her father's influence. She supposed that meant being free of Rafe's influence, as well.

And after tonight, she would be. At least, that was the hope.

But this kiss didn't taste like freedom. It tasted like deep, crushing need. Like willing bondage. Like she was committing herself to him again with each pass of her tongue against his.

But she couldn't do that. She couldn't. If she was going to take this night, then she had to be committed to her plan. To her freedom.

Freedom was the one thing she'd never had. Her life on her own terms. She couldn't steal it from herself. Not before she had ever had a chance to hold it in her hands.

But she had never had a chance to hold him either. And now it seemed imperative. Necessary. Like the thing she needed more than air...

He bit her bottom lip and desire arrowed down

straight to her stomach, down farther between her legs. She remembered this. It had rested in the back of her mind, a half-faded memory for five years. But now it was back. Bright, sharp and clear.

This thing that she had felt only ever with him. This thing that was like a wild, untamed beast inside of her. The only thing that ever was. The only thing that ever had been.

She had been hidden away, kept apart from the world on the estate, locked away from the world in a tower. And the only wild, untamed thing in her had always been for him.

It was astonishing how true that was now. How quickly she was transported back to that time. To her bedroom. When the only good and wonderful thing in her life had been Rafe. He had been worth everything. Worth risks she knew both of them took great pains not to dwell on.

They had of course spoken of the need for them not to get caught. But it had been like children sneaking around. Rather than two people who were in very real danger should they ever be discovered.

But there was no one to discover them now. There was no danger. Those things that had made it feel all the more special, forbidden, were gone now. There were no walls. No one was in chains, so to speak. They were here of their own free will. Making this choice.

She was not the only available body that he might find pleasure in. She was not a trapped girl who had met no other men that appealed to her.

No, she hadn't dated anyone but they just hadn't called to her. Not in the way that Rafe did.

No one ever had. No one.

She reached up, ready to unpin her hair, which he had always liked. Something he had always asked of her.

He gripped her wrist. "No."

"But—"

"There will be none of that. Leave it up."

Those words scraped her raw. Left her wounded. She couldn't quite fathom why. Except that maybe, no matter what he had said, he didn't want to be so conscious that it was her. He couldn't see her, after all. And asking her to keep her hair up was truly like asking her to stay shrouded in darkness.

She would have to decide, she supposed, if that wounded her enough to make her walk out.

No. It didn't. Because this wasn't about her. It wasn't about her feelings. It certainly wasn't about trying to recapture something that had happened between them long ago. This was a step forward. The closing of the door. She had to allow it to be that.

She had to allow it to be unique. Its own experience. And if he wanted to keep her hair up, then that was fine by her.

Her hair was another thing that had had far too much importance attached to it for far too long.

Maybe that would be another change she would make when all this was done.

She had left it unchanged for all these years, after all. And she knew why. It had nothing to do with her father. As Rafe had said long ago, her father's obsession with it had been nothing short of creepy.

This was for Rafe. Her hair was for Rafe. He had loved uncoiling it from its bun, loved wrapping it around his hand. Loved running his fingers through the silken strands. She had left it for him. For five years, she had left it.

Perhaps when this was over, she would not feel that compulsion.

Clearly, he didn't require it of her anyway.

"Take your clothes off," he said, his words cutting through the silence like a knife, slicing straight down into her soul.

She hesitated. Only for a breath.

"All right." She reached around behind her back, and gripped hold of the zipper tab.

"I want you to tell me what you were wearing," he said, speaking slowly. With supreme authority.

"To…to tell you?" she asked, the words choked.

"Yes. Tell me in great detail exactly what you were wearing tonight. A gown, I assume, and with an interesting material. Not silken. A thin layer over something heavier. Yes?"

"Yes," she confirmed.

"Describe it to me as you remove it."

He was standing in the center of the room, his expression impassive, his dark eyes resting behind her. Even if he had been looking directly at her, she knew that he wouldn't be able to see.

"It's…it's red," she began haltingly. She started to try to jerk the zipper down, but it was as halting as her words. "It has a V-neck, thin straps. It conforms to my figure. Hugs my hips. And follows my body closely all the way down past my knees. It flares out there. Like a mermaid's tail."

"Very interesting. And what is underneath this gown?"

She let the straps fall around her waist, a whispering noise as it fell away from her curves and pooled at her feet.

"Underneath…" She swallowed hard. "My bra is red. It matches the gown. It's made of lace."

"I see. And would I be able to see those beautiful nipples through it? They were very pale. I recall that clearly. All of you is very pale. Your nipples...they are a particular shade of pink that I find extremely arousing. Like candy. It makes my mouth water just thinking about it."

She swallowed hard, trembling now. "Yes. You would be able to see them."

"If I could see," he said, his tone dark.

"Yes," she said softly. "If you could see."

"Please tell me that your underwear matches. That they are red and lacy, and that I would be able to see your beautiful golden curls through the fabric."

She could hardly breathe. She felt dizzy.

"Yes." She swallowed hard again. "The fabric is transparent."

She had never played the part of seductress. Those weeks in her room *he* had been seducing *her*. And while she had certainly begged him to take things further—to take them all the way— he had still been the one in control of the situation. It felt different now. The air between them an electric shock. And his expression... Growing tighter, growing more tense as the moments wore on. His hands were curled into fists at his side, and he might have been made of stone.

Beautiful stone that looked as though it would be hot to the touch. There was a strange power in this moment. In him demanding that she paint a picture in his mind. She could have told him anything, but she found that she wanted nothing more than to give him honesty. Because here, in this strong man, was some sense of vulnerability. He was stronger than her. More experienced than her. As he had always been.

But she had some power. She did.

Because he had given it to her.

Even now, with things as they were between them, he had handed her this.

"I want you to remove the bra," he commanded.

Without thought, she obeyed.

"Now tell me," he said, his voice rough now. "Are your nipples tight? From the cold air? From my voice? From your arousal? Knowing exactly what I will do next. Because you know me, and you know I am insatiable when it comes to those breasts of yours. I'm going to suck one of those sweet buds into my mouth, lick you, taste you."

She shivered. "Yes."

"Yes, you want me to taste you? Or yes, they are tight?"

"Both," she whispered, the word husky, her voice unrecognizable as her own.

A smile curved his mouth, and she would be tempted to describe it as cruel.

"The panties next. Push them down your hips slowly." He smiled wider. "You did not tell me about your shoes."

"Stilettos. Red. Like the dress."

"And are you still wearing them?"

"You didn't tell me to take them off yet."

His mouth twitched. "Good. Leave them on."

She complied with his wishes, pushing the thin scrap of fabric down her legs slowly, then kicking them off to the side. And she prepared for more commands.

"Now tell me," he said, his voice like gravel. "Are you wet for me? There between your thighs, are you wet and aching for my touch? You have been touched by me there before. Remember. How I would put my hand between your legs and stroke you, draw the moisture out from inside of you and rub my thumb over your clit? Do you remember that?"

"Yes," she answered in a rush.

"And is that what you want from me now? My tongue sliding through those slick folds? My fingers deep inside you?"

She had tried. On more than one occasion to replicate the kind of pleasure he had given her with his hands with her own. It was never the same. It didn't work like that. She hadn't felt that kind of pleasure in five long years. And what he was saying now went beyond this kind of elevated need for closure. All of these excuses she had been giving herself. Yes, this went far beyond that.

This was just about want. Pure, undiluted sexual need. Something she thought she had lost touch with.

But apparently, Rafe had simply been holding on to it for safekeeping.

"I want that."

"Good." He turned away from her. "You can leave the shoes on. And I want you to walk with me to my bedroom."

CHAPTER FOUR

HE BLAZED THE trail to the room, and she followed, her high heels clicking on the glossy marble floor.

He pushed the door open, revealing a large, pristinely made bed that took her breath away. Because they would be in that bed together. And there would be nothing stopping them this time. Nothing stopping them from consummating this need that had blazed between them for so long.

Before there had always been something else. Always something stopping them. Some kind of obstacle. But that was gone now. There was no need to stop. No pretense available.

She sucked in a sharp breath and walked toward the bed, standing at the foot of it.

"Where are you?" he asked.

"Just in front of the bed. At the foot of it."

He oriented himself, then walked toward her. Following her voice and her instructions unerringly.

"What color is your lipstick? I hope it's red. Red like everything else."

Her heart slammed against her breastbone. "It is."

"I want it all over my body," he rasped. "I want you to be able to see exactly what has happened between us. Come here."

She complied, taking two steps to close the distance between them.

"Kiss me," he demanded. "Right here." He lifted his hand and pointed to his neck. Just at his throat. She leaned forward, pressed a slow, firm kiss to his skin there.

She moved away, looking up at him.

"Have you left a mark?"

She surveyed her work, the red smudge left behind on his skin. "Yes."

"Good." A muscle in his jaw ticked. "Now. You will undress me next. Start with my jacket. Then my tie. Then my shirt."

Charlotte felt dizzy and breathless, but desperate to obey. She pushed his jacket from his shoulders, not caring where it landed. Then she undid his tie, the black silk sliding easily to the floor.

With unsteady hands, she undid the top button on his shirt, then pressed her fingertips tentatively to his chest, and then leaned in, kissing him there, just above his heart. "I've marked you there too," she said softly.

She undid the next button, then moved lower. The next button. And she followed the path, moving lower still, inhaling the scent of his skin. And then, she was lost in memory. Because this was still Rafe as she remembered him. She had unbuttoned his shirt many times.

Had seen him naked.

Yes, he was more heavily muscled now, with more hair on his chest. But he was still Rafe. And she *remembered* this. Remembered him.

The way his skin tasted. How starving she was for him all the time. How she couldn't get enough.

She untucked his shirt from his pants, spreading it wide, then kissed him, just above his belt before taking hold of it with trembling fingers and working it through the buckle. She had done this before. For him. She had forced him to accept it, actually. Because while he was playing the part of chivalrous knight, pleasuring her in various ways without technically taking her virginity, he had taken nothing for himself.

And so she had insisted. And once she had started, he had not been able to stop her. More accurately, she didn't believe he had wanted to.

He had played at honor back then, or at least at control, but he had certainly enjoyed surrendering it to her when she had gotten down on her knees. She hoped it would be the same now.

She pushed his pants and underwear down his hips, revealing that hard pillar of masculinity. Her heart thundered, her entire body seizing up tight. She remembered this too. Remembered him. The shape of him. The way he had felt in her hand. Hard, hot and endlessly enticing.

She reached up, curving her fingers around his hardened length and letting out a long, slow sigh of satisfaction. He jerked beneath her touch, and she smiled. And suddenly, the years melted away. As she leaned forward, sliding her tongue over him before taking him deep into her mouth, it was easy to imagine that she was back in her tower room during one of their hot, illicit nights.

He reached down, gripping her hair, which was still firmly coiled in the heavy bun at the back of her head. And that reminded her. The sharp tug bringing her back to reality, the realization that her hair was bound. That reminded her that this was not five years ago. And they were not the Rafe and Charlotte that they had once been.

That filled her with an unaccountable sadness. But on the heels of it came a strong sense of empowerment. Because she had as much power here as he did. Because there was nothing looming over them. They had this night. All night.

For anything—everything—that they wanted.

After so long, she was essentially made of want. She would take every last one of the hours before them to satisfy it. She gripped the base of his shaft and took him deeper, and he tugged harder on her hair, pulling her mouth away from him.

"Enough of that," he said. "This, I have had from you."

"And somehow...you're tired of it?"

He pressed his thumb to the center of her bottom lip. "I will have your mouth on me later. Believe me. But for now, I wish to be inside you." He paused for a moment, tilting his head to the side. "Have you left lipstick there, as well?"

Her cheeks heated, and she examined him. "Yes."

He growled, a feral, untamed sound, and bent down, wrapping his arm around her waist and hauling her up against him. Then, he walked them both backward, tumbling with her onto the bed.

The rest of his clothes, and both of their shoes, were discarded onto the floor, and he kissed her like he was a lost soul on his way to hell and she might provide the necessary ingredient to his salvation.

"You're so soft," he said, abandoning her lips

to press a kiss to the tender skin on the side of her neck. "So warm. I imagine you are flushed from arousal. I remember how you used to do that. Your pale skin turning pink, starting at your cheeks and moving down your neck." He pressed his thumb against her pulse again. "Yes. And your heart would beat fast, just like this. And then..." He moved his hand down to cup her bare breast, that deft thumb of his sliding over her nipple. "Yes. Your nipples were always so responsive. So tight. Just for me."

She gasped as he pinched her lightly, then replaced his hand with his mouth, flicking the tightened bud with his tongue before sucking her in deep.

It was a sensory overload. After so many years without physical contact, it was almost too much. But he was merciless, and when she let out a sob that was wrenched from deep within her body, one she could not have controlled if she had wanted to, rather than easing off, he pressed his fingers between her legs, pushing through her slick folds.

His thumb moved in a circular motion over her clit as he pushed his middle finger inside her and she saw stars. Then, he added a second finger, the fullness unfamiliar. He had never done this before. Part of sparing her innocence and all of that. But there was none of that happening tonight.

Thankfully.

She closed her eyes, letting her head fall back. And she ignored the uncomfortable lump created by her restrained mass of hair. Ignored the pins digging into her scalp. She didn't care about any of that. Didn't care about anything but the intensity of the pleasure burning through her like a wildfire.

Orgasm was closing in on her; she knew it. But she wanted to hold it off for as long as possible. Wanted to exist on this knife's edge until she couldn't possibly stand it any longer. That was what she had wanted back then too. To extend her time with him. Because once she was satisfied, he would leave. Lingering too long a risk that neither of them could take. And so she had learned to hold back. To find pleasure in the exquisite torture that came with denying herself release.

In the interest of having Rafe's hands on her for longer. In the interest of staying lost. Of no longer existing as Charlotte Adair, daughter of a notorious crime lord, but as a creature made entirely of pleasure. Of need.

But it had been so long. And it was too much. She couldn't bear to hold it off, not for one more moment. And so she gave in. Diving deep into that pool of pleasure, into that release that only Rafe had ever given her. She was breathless. Weightless. Thoughtless for an extended space of time. Made of nothing but deep, pulsing satisfaction that pounded through her like waves on the rocks.

When her release ended she looked up at Rafe. His eyes were closed.

Then he lifted his hand to his lips, and sucked the two fingers that had just been inside her into his mouth. Fire, white hot and savage, burned through her. She wasn't sure if it was shame or if it was need on a level she had never known before. Certainly, there was embarrassment, because that had been such a base and carnal act.

And yet, she understood it. Because hadn't she been compelled to taste him? As she had once done. She wanted more than a few quick strokes of her tongue. She wanted all of him. But he was right. There would be time for that later.

He grabbed hold of her legs and parted them, kneeling before her, that most masculine part of him standing out from his body, thick and proud, and for the very first time—intimidating.

Every other time she had been with him there had been no expectation that he would be inside her the way he was about to be.

She had always enjoyed the shape of him. The way he had felt in her hand.

And somewhat foolishly she had imagined there would be no virginal nerves tonight. Because wasn't she familiar with his body? Hadn't they been naked together many times before? She'd had him in her mouth, had brought him pleasure with her hand. It had given her a false sense of experience.

One she certainly did not feel now.

He reached down, cupping her cheek, his fingers curving around the back of her head as he lifted her from the mattress, claiming her mouth with his own. He brought her up against his body, wrapping her legs around his waist, bringing his hardness right up against the place where she ached for him the most.

He wrapped his other arm around her waist, his hold like iron. Her breasts were crushed against his chest, and she could feel his heart raging. And somehow, that calmed her nerves. The realization that he felt all of this too. He might look hard, unaffected and utterly composed, but his body told another story entirely.

There was no more talking. There were no more commands. There was just raw, unleashed desire, poured out onto her body like an anointing.

He slid his hand down to her lower back, then lower still, grabbing hold of her rear and squeezing her tight as he lifted her against him, the head of his shaft finding the entrance to her body.

She couldn't breathe. She began to protest. To say something about how she wasn't ready. How she didn't think she could take all of him, at least not without taking it slowly. But before she could, he tilted his hips forward, then pushed hard into her body, filling her in one breathtaking thrust.

It hurt. Her eyes watered, and she bit her lip hard and waited for the stinging sensation to subside. It didn't take long. Because she was so slick, and because there was something delicious about the way that he filled her, even if it was unfamiliar and painful.

A great many things in life were painful, and they weren't anywhere near this beautiful. She would take this pain gladly. Because finally she was joined to Rafe. The way that she had always dreamed of.

He was frozen. His face like granite, his unseeing eyes like ice. But he said nothing. Then, finally he closed his eyes, letting his head fall back. Slowly, without withdrawing from her, he laid her down onto the mattress, rolling his hips forward and going deeper—impossibly so—as he lowered his head and kissed her lips gently.

But the only gentleness came in that moment. And in the space of a breath, it was gone.

He reached down, gripping her hips and holding her steady as he thrust hard against her. She closed her eyes, and she saw stars. She was glad. She didn't want this to be a slow, easy coupling. Because they had never been slow or easy. The last five years seemed to shrink, and they disappeared altogether as his body met hers, fast, furious and deep.

She gripped his shoulders, her fingernails digging into his back, while his blunt fingertips were certainly making bruises in her pale skin. It was what she wanted. To be marked by this. Changed in a way that was visible.

So that tomorrow when she went back to the apartment she had just signed the papers for, the place that would be hers, and she looked in the mirror she would be able to see the changes in her body with just a glance.

She wanted to be sore between her thighs. Wanted to see the impression of his hands, where he had held on to her. She wanted to be wrecked by this. Ruined. So that she could rise from those ashes, instead of simply appearing quietly, meekly, from hiding.

He whispered things in her ear, dark and rough, in his native Italian. Words she didn't know. Words she had never heard. Which certainly ensured that they were dirty.

That sent a thrill through her body. Twisted that coil of arousal that was starting low in her stomach again, heightening it all. She moved her hands from his shoulders, sliding them up his neck, gripping his face firmly, and holding it steady, bringing his head down so that his forehead was pressed hard against hers.

She kept her eyes open, forced herself to bear witness to this. Because he couldn't.

Even so, those dark eyes bore through her. And she could almost swear that though he couldn't see the features on her face, he might be able to see into her soul.

The rhythm between them was frantic, desperate. And she clung to him as she lost herself in it. In him.

She pressed her lips to his, and then began to say things. Things she didn't understand any more than the Italian he had just spoken to her. Desperate demands, promises. Supplication. She spoke words to him she had never said out loud in her life, begging for more. Begging for him.

It wasn't just the way it felt physically. Being connected to him... It was more than that. It didn't satisfy a need; it simply unveiled how deep her need was. To be connected to someone else. To be needed. To need in return.

Pleasure stretched inside her like a wire, drawing tight from her lungs, down to her toes. She had the sense that it was holding her together. That when it snapped, she would fly apart, never to be put back together again.

Just like before, she fought against it. Fought against the end. But she could feel her hold on her control slipping. Could feel her mind starting to get hazy, her thoughts going fuzzy. It was hard to remember why she wanted to hold off her pleasure in the first place. Difficult to grasp on to where she was, and why she was afraid for the end to come.

But she never forgot who she was with.

It was Rafe. It could only ever have been Rafe.

And then he growled, his teeth digging into the cords on her neck as he began to slam into her, no consideration, no gentleness remaining at all. And she rejoiced. Letting go. Just as he had done.

She turned her face, curving it into his shoulder as she rode out the impossible release that flooded through her. There had never been anything like this. Like losing control with him.

They had traded pleasure in her room. Her hand, then his. His mouth, then hers. But they had never gone over together like this. She had never felt him pulsing inside her as he spilled himself.

It was everything. It was perfect.

It was finished. At least, that was the idea.

This was supposed to be the ultimate fulfillment. The satisfaction that she had been waiting for for the past five years. And yet, as soon as the storm passed, she wanted more. She wanted him.

He moved away from her, rolling onto his back, breathing hard. "Would you care to explain that?"

"I wouldn't have thought you would need the facts of life explained to you at this point, Rafe," she commented, feeling the need to put up some kind of shield between them. Because she felt so vulnerable. So exposed. Naked. When before it had all felt easy.

"That," he bit out, "is not what I meant. And you know it."

"We have amazing chemistry," she responded. "But we've always known that. We risked our health and safety to explore it, if you recall."

"I take it you are unmarried."

She frowned. And then she remembered that he had mentioned her husband back at the ball. It had all grown hazy in the interim. By the revelation that they'd been lied to by her father and stepmother. And then it had been lost in the pleasure.

It was incredibly distracting pleasure.

"I'm not. You assumed that I was. I never said either way. And frankly, with everything else going on I didn't really...think of it."

"And you were a virgin."

"The last five years haven't exactly been an ascent to success for *me*."

He chuckled, the sound hard and dark. "In contrast, they have been a walk in the park for me."

"I'm sorry," she said. "That was thoughtless of me. I escaped."

She looked over at him, and he was frowning. "You escaped?"

"My father kidnapped me and attempted to sell me into marriage, Rafe. When I refused to go willingly even after I was told that you had left me. I suppose they thought without you there I would have no reason to resist. Shockingly, I took exception to being married off to a crime lord. Fancy that."

Rafe pushed himself into a sitting position, his muscles rippling. "Your father tried to sell you into marriage?"

"You look surprised, Rafe. We are talking

about a man that we hid our romance from so that he would not kill us both."

"And yet, in the end they clearly knew. And opted not to kill either of us."

She nodded. "I never quite figured that out."

"In my case I know that it was due in part to the fact that eventually I became too high profile." There was something strange and opaque in those words. But right now, her brain was scrambled, and she couldn't quite parse it.

"And you left."

"When I was told you had opted to marry another man I did not see why I should stay," he said, clipped.

"But I didn't. I was carted off. And I escaped. I have spent the past five years hiding. So, the opposite tactic to you. You became more visible. While I faded into invisibility. An easy thing to do, all things considered. You know, since I had spent all of my previous years hidden away at the villa."

His expression was utterly black. Terrifying. "If your father were not dead, I would kill him myself. And that is one of the very few sins I have never committed."

"He wouldn't have been worth it. It wouldn't have been worth destroying yourself for." She blinked, her eyes filling with tears. "It doesn't matter. We're free of him now."

"Yes. And we still have the rest of the night."

Her heart squeezed tight, need filling her. "Yes." She leaned in, kissing him on the mouth. "We do."

And after this, she would find herself. After this, she would find her freedom.

Finally. This was the end.

The end they both needed. So they could finally have a beginning that they chose for themselves.

CHAPTER FIVE

"DID YOU GET the report I asked for?"

It had been weeks since Charlotte had walked out of his penthouse and out of his life, yet again. It had been part of their agreement this time. Still, Rafe felt unsettled. He told himself it was because he was concerned for her safety. After all, she had been living in cottages in the woods and small villages for the past five years. She had not been trying to navigate London.

Why he should care, he didn't know. Except, he felt differently about her now, knowing that she had not abandoned him. Though, guilt was a new companion. He had taken her stepmother at her word.

Yet pursuing her would have been difficult. It had taken him months to heal from his injuries. And then, there were those that had never fully healed. By then, he had been certain that she was settled into her new life.

And he could think of nothing sadder than playing the part of injured, rejected boyfriend crawling after the woman who had willingly left him.

But he should have known. He should have.

"Yes, Mr. Costa. I got the files that you asked for, though it seems to me that a great deal of this is a violation of privacy laws."

Rafe sighed heavily as he shifted the phone from one ear to the other. "Undoubtedly. But that is not my concern. And anyway, that is why I paid for a third party to acquire the information and not you, Alyssa."

"Well, it is all here. Shall I put together an email for you?"

"If you please."

Rafe ended the call with his assistant and turned toward the office window, which he had been told offered an expansive view of London. The Thames. The London Eye. Big Ben and the Abbey. A view such as this spoke of status. Of security. It was only the mortals that had to stand below and view bits and pieces of these icons rather than taking in the full reality of the city.

He couldn't see it; that was true. But it was there. He took a perverse amount of pride in that. In the fact he owned this view and had never even seen it.

It spoke of excess in a way that appeased him. Spoke of his power. As did his ability to keep tabs on Charlotte. Now that she was not in hiding, she was doing a very poor job of not leaving a paper trail.

He had obtained her address easily enough, and he had asked for his contact to keep him apprised of any other information about her that might be relevant. Anything that went into an online system that he could find a back door into.

Rafe loved technology. He had built his fortune on it. But more than that, he adored how it had such fatally flawed weak points. When everything was in hard copy it was much easier to keep secure. But the moment something was put out on a network…it had the potential to be exposed. To be obtained by those who were never supposed to see it.

His mobile phone buzzed, and he gritted his teeth in annoyance when the ringtone kicked in—the specific tone he had set for his friend, Prince Felipe. His Royal Highness and general pain in Rafe's ass.

He sighed, and then answered. "To what do I owe the pleasure?" Rafe asked, not meaning it at all.

"Hang on for just a second," Felipe said.

"*You* called *me*," Rafe said, his patience feeling stretched. But then, it had been feeling severely compromised from the moment Charlotte had walked out of his penthouse.

"I did. But I'm also calling Adam."

Prince Adam Katsaros had been his other friend at the private school he had been sent to by Michael Adair. It had been his happiest time. A time when he had been on his own, but had also possessed the resources that he needed to survive.

Of course, it had come with a price. The price

of his indentured servitude. At the time, it had seemed reasonable.

"Hello?" Adam came on the line.

"Excellent," Felipe said. "I wanted to ask Rafe if he would fill us in on who the woman was that he was spotted leaving a party with some weeks ago."

Rafe gritted his teeth. "That's what you want to know? Why are you calling me now? Why didn't you call me weeks ago?"

"Because I *want* something from you now," Felipe said. "And I'm not one to waste a phone call."

"That isn't true," Adam said. "You are one to waste several phone calls. And a great many words."

"Your opinion is fascinating," Felipe said. "My wife finds me delightful."

"Then it's a good thing she married you instead of one of us," Rafe said drily. "Now, get to the point."

"Briar is spearheading an art exhibition in a couple of months. And I wanted to make sure that it was appropriately populated with my very influential friends. It is a showcase of my country's work. And also of her first original works. Now. All of you must come or the next time you do come to visit me I will throw you in the dungeon."

"I see no problem with it. Though, I find my enjoyment of art is somewhat truncated these days," Rafe said.

"Yes, but your enjoyment of beautiful women is suddenly not. A notable change from the past few years, is it not?" Felipe pressed.

"All signs point to it," Adam supplied.

"Perhaps you should both be concerned more with your marriages than with my sex life?"

"We worry about you," Felipe said, "because we are true friends."

Rafe mumbled something about friends being overrated. Then a tone went off on his computer, and he made his way back to his desk. He muted the microphone on his call, then gave his computer voice instructions to read his email to him.

The file was lengthy. His Charlotte had been busy.

He continued to half listen to Adam and Felipe

talk logistics in terms of the exhibit in Felipe's country.

But his attention fell away from that as he continued to listen to the contents of his file regarding Charlotte. She had gone to the bank. She had secured a large sum of money. He had access to everything. Her balance, the account it had been transferred from. It surprised him to know that her father had left some money in a trust for her.

He wondered if the old man had forgotten about it. If it had actually been a way for him to hide some of his money. Money he had intended to move before he died. If he knew one thing about Charlotte's father, it was that he had certainly fancied himself immortal in many respects. He most definitely wouldn't have thought his death would come so soon.

There were mundane things in there too. Receipts for online shopping. Uninteresting. She had bought a table lamp. And oven mitts.

Then there was the last bit of information. She had made a doctor's appointment. At a private women's health clinic.

It was entirely possible that it was for a regular checkup. Entirely possible.

But it had been weeks since they were together. And the first time they had not used a condom. He hadn't been thinking straight, and neither had she. She had also been a virgin—something he hadn't counted on. But that led him to assume that she had not been on any kind of birth control.

A women's health clinic. The implications of that pounded their way through him like a battering ram. Felipe was still talking, but Rafe was past the point of listening.

The appointment was this afternoon. And the address was on the paperwork. He had just over an hour to get across the city, and he would be damned if he was going to miss it.

"I have to go. I will be at your party—don't worry." He hung up the phone, and he quickly buzzed for his secretary. "Get my helicopter ready."

Charlotte walked into the clinic with clammy hands. Her heart was pounding hard, and she could scarcely breathe. She had taken about ten home pregnancy tests, so it wasn't as if she expected to get any other news here at the appointment. But of course, this would be real confirmation.

It was hugely expensive to book an early scan at a place like this, but she didn't have a GP, and there was a long waiting list to get in at the hospital, so she'd just done a quick online search and decided to throw some of her father's money at a private women's clinic.

If she really was pregnant with Rafe's baby, spending her father's money to confirm it was amusing in some ways. Even if nothing else about the situation was.

She could tell herself whatever she wanted about being under stress, about life changes affecting her cycle. But the fact of the matter was she had gone on the lam for five years, constantly afraid that somebody might find her, and had never once missed a period. Most likely, it had more to do with the fact that she had had sex for the first time in her life, and it had been unprotected. Something she had blocked out of her mind the moment she had walked away from Rafe's penthouse.

She checked in at the front desk and then walked into the plush waiting room. And her heart nearly exploded.

Because there he was. In the clinic. It wasn't possible. It didn't seem like it could be. She had spent five years running from one of the criminal world's most notorious bosses, and no one had found her.

But Rafe was here. He was here, and he had to know.

"What are you doing here?" she asked.

He turned toward the sound of her voice. "I would ask you the same question, but I have a strong suspicion that I already know."

"I'm here for a Pap smear," she said, staring him down.

"I doubt that."

"Ms. Adair." She turned to see a nurse standing in the doorway. "Dr. Schultz is ready to see you now."

"I will be accompanying her," Rafe said, standing up from his chair. He grabbed hold of his cane, black with a silver tip, and began to walk toward where the nurse was.

"You will certainly not accompany me," Charlotte said, keeping her voice low.

He moved toward her then, much more quickly than she expected him to. "Do not make a scene, *cara mia*," he said. "You will not like the way it ends."

She was too numb to protest further. She should have. She should have screamed and tipped over the ficus by the door. Then, maybe someone would have stopped him. But who would have? Who was going to physically accost Rafe Costa, known billionaire and powerful businessman? And even if they didn't know who he was, he was well over six feet tall and made almost entirely of muscle.

Charlotte imagined that she wouldn't find an ally here.

Her temples were pounding as they walked down the hallway that Charlotte assumed would lead to the exam room. She felt like the walls were closing in on her. Like the sky might be crushing down on her.

And she had to ask herself why she had been so desperate to keep this from Rafe in the first place. It was his baby. There was no one else. There never had been.

That initial response, the one that had demanded that she keep all of this to herself, had been based in panic. He was here now. Didn't he deserve to know?

Her own father had played the part of villain in her life; that much was true. But Rafe wasn't a villain. She knew that.

Maybe there would be no baby. That would be a good thing. She was only just beginning to figure out what she wanted after a lifetime of being hidden away.

She was only just beginning to figure out who Charlotte Adair was. On her own. Without a group of men searching for her. She had no idea what she would do if she was supposed to try to figure that out while trying to figure out how to be a mother.

She had never even held a baby. There had never been any children at her father's compound except for her.

Yes, she had watched women push strollers around when she'd worked at the shops. She had watched them kiss away fat, angry tears from chubby cheeks. And of course, she had wondered what it must be like. To have someone to love. Someone who would love you so very much in return.

The thought made her chest ache. But her head hurt too. From the impossibility of all of this.

And then there was Rafe. Who loomed large behind her.

She was handed a small plastic cup and directed toward a bathroom. Her cheeks flamed as she went inside. And then she tried not to think about the fact that Rafe knew exactly what the cup was for as she completed the task.

She exited the restroom and went into the

exam room. And the nurse left Rafe and Charlotte alone.

"When exactly were you going to tell me?" he asked as soon as the door had closed behind the retreating nurse.

"I was definitely going to wait until I had something confirmed by a professional. When you think about it, it's a little bit ridiculous that we're supposed to buy something from a grocery store that tells us something so essential, and just trust that it's correct."

"I see. And how many of those did you take?"

She waved a hand. "I don't know. Maybe ten?"

"I see." His jaw was hard, his face set into a grim expression. "And what did those ten tests tell you, Charlotte?"

"That I'm pregnant," she answered, feeling subdued.

There was a knock on the door, and Dr. Schultz swept into the room. After some risk preparation, Charlotte found herself staring at an ultrasound screen as the Doppler swept over her stomach.

"There isn't much to see at this stage," Dr.

Schultz said, her eyes on the screen. "But we do want to confirm viability."

"What do you see?" Rafe asked, from his position in the corner.

"Nothing yet," the doctor said.

"Just black lines," Charlotte said softly.

Then the image on the screen changed. And she could see it. Just ever so faintly. A little bit of motion.

Charlotte couldn't help it. She giggled. The strangest response she could have imagined having to such a thing.

"What?" Rafe asked.

"Something moved," Charlotte said, looking up at the doctor.

"Yes," Dr. Schultz responded, changing something on the ultrasound machine, turning up the sound so that a watery noise filled the room. And beneath the kind of indistinct blur was a rhythmic whispering. "That's a heartbeat."

Charlotte looked over at Rafe, who had gone pale. And then a second, very similar sound filled the room.

Charlotte's head whipped back toward the screen. She looked up at the doctor. "Is that…?"

"That is a second heartbeat," the doctor responded. "Congratulations. Twins."

The words were ringing in Rafe's ears after the doctor left, and Charlotte was dressing. He could hear her rustling in the corner. She was otherwise silent.

The black hell that he lived in seemed to close in around him. His sense of the slight distinction between light and dark felt erased in that moment.

Twins. Charlotte was having twins.

And he—a man who had never had a father, a man who had no sense of how to be a father—was supposed to know what to do.

He couldn't see. He would never see his children. How would he care for them?

With nannies. Of course. That's the purpose of money.

He heard a sharp movement from Charlotte's

direction. And that was when he realized he had spoken those dour words out loud.

"I doubt I'll need nannies," she said, her voice stiff.

"Did you not care for yours?" He had rather liked his. What he could remember of her.

He had spent only five years in that life. The life where there had been shining marble halls and nannies and all the food he could want. But he'd been happy then. As far as he recalled.

She huffed out a laugh. "On the contrary, they were an improvement to my father and step-mother. I imagine that perhaps my mother was fine enough. But I know nothing about her since she died in childbirth, and my father never spoke of her. I always got the impression that Josefina was his mistress before my mother's passing. All she did was change rooms. And gain an official title."

"So, then nannies are not so bad."

"But I won't need them. I will need to work at some point because the money that my father left me—whether he left it intentionally or not—won't last forever, but it will be sufficient for a time."

"You seem resolved."

"I am," she responded, taking a couple of steps toward him, wearing hard-soled shoes that made a distinct sound as she moved.

He cursed his lack of sight yet again. Because he would like very much to be able to see how she was reacting, truthfully. Not just with her brave, carefully chosen words. He wanted to see her face. If she was pale. If she looked as frightened as he suspected she probably was.

His whole life was structured to serve him, and he rarely thought much about his lost vision. But Charlotte—this piece of his past that she represented—brought out memories. Memories of what it had been like to hold her in his arms, to look at her pale body, to brush his fingers through her golden hair.

Visions of how she had looked standing in an open field with the overwhelming light of the sun pouring over her beauty, illuminating her.

And that brought out the contrast of what it was

like to be with her now and to be robbed of that vision. To have this future—children—looming before him and yet to see nothing more than darkness.

"I am resolved, as well." He stood, walking across the space between them and holding out his hand. He could sense her hesitation. "Please take my hand," he said. "I am in unfamiliar surroundings, and it would be helpful."

While that was not strictly untrue, it wasn't really true either.

She took his hand, and he allowed her to lead him toward the door, which he could have found on his own.

"Did you take a cab to get here?"

"Yes," she responded. "I don't feel all that well and I didn't want the hassle of the Tube."

"I never do. But then, I rarely bother with traffic. Where do you need to go?"

"Home," she said simply.

She was not going home. He was resolved about that. And he was done at the office for the day. But he wasn't going to tell her that.

"I have a helicopter. Do you suppose it's possible to land on your building?"

He could tell by the resounding silence beside him that he had succeeded in shocking her. He was gratified by that. "You know, I didn't ask about helicopter parking when I moved in."

"An oversight."

"You don't need to give me a...flight back."

"Allow me to. My pilot will know exactly where he can land that's in proximity to your building." It didn't actually matter.

"Rafe..."

"I am told the view of London is quite spectacular. Of course, I am not able to see it. It would be nice if one of us could enjoy it."

Had he a conscience remaining inside him that was something other than a theoretical understanding of right and wrong, he might have felt guilty about that. But he didn't. So he didn't.

She sighed heavily. "All right. I'll let you give me a ride back. I've never been in a helicopter before. I've never flown before."

"Are you nervous?"

"No." She sounded somewhat astonished by that. "I'm not."

They went up to the top of the building, where the helicopter was waiting for them, and he allowed her to brace herself on his hand as she got into the vehicle. He followed suit, putting on his headset and holding hers back as the rotor started turning, creating a deafening sound around them.

He knew that she wouldn't be able to hear the instructions he was giving to his pilot.

"To the castle," he said.

Then he handed Charlotte her own headset. She would figure it all out soon enough. When the flight took them over the ocean, and took more than an hour. But unless she was going to fling herself from the helicopter—and he doubted it— by then it would be too late.

It took a while. He wasn't quite certain what the view below looked like, but he had made the educated assumption that they were leaving London behind when Charlotte spoke.

"My flat is the other direction," she said.

"I like your English," he said. "An interesting

mixture. American in some ways. Vaguely British in others. If I recall correctly, your Italian is quite good too."

"Wonderful. But that has nothing to do with what I just said."

"Because I'm not concerned about what you just said."

"You're not concerned about the fact that your pilot might be lost?"

"My pilot is not lost. He's going exactly where I told him to go."

"Where...where did you tell him to go?"

"Why, we're going to my castle in Germany, *cara mia*."

"I just escaped Germany," she said sharply. "Why would I want to go back?"

"You seemed to have fond memories of it. It is incredible to me that we spent some time in the same country and never knew it." He settled back in his seat, feeling more and more relaxed as the journey wore on. Because he had already won. "I heard about a castle for sale and simply couldn't resist it. After all, my two closest friends are royalty, and I didn't want to be left out."

"What difference does it make? You can't even see it."

She spat the words, and they hit him like a slap. He quite liked it. Enjoyed the fact that she was strong even though she had been raised by a madman who would as soon have used her as a pawn to shore up his empire as given her a hug.

"Yes, but it pleases me to know what surrounds me. Anyway, you must know a castle possesses a certain atmosphere. It cannot be replicated by a modern building. In fact, I would suggest to you that such atmosphere is more important to someone such as myself than it would be to someone like you. I can feel the history when I walk through the doors. I can smell the age of the rooms. The books. Everything in modern construction is so smooth. It lacks texture. In the castle... It is everywhere. I can feel how the walls look."

"Why are you taking me there?"

"Because," he said. "I find I have lost quite

enough in my life to risk losing my children, as well. You weren't going to tell me. I think we both know that. Why, I cannot fathom. I thought we had come to some sort of agreement, some sort of understanding. I didn't abandon you, any more than you abandoned me. And yet, you're still treating me like a man you have reason to distrust."

"He says as he kidnaps me *in a helicopter.*"

Rafe chuckled and leaned back in his seat. "But I hadn't kidnapped you before."

"You worked for my father. You know what that says about you."

"You didn't mind when you were eighteen and letting me put my hands between your legs. And you certainly didn't mind a few weeks ago when you begged for my—"

"Stop it," she hissed.

"You and I will have plenty of time to talk over the next few months. So for now, I will stop. Because later...later you and I will reckon with each other. That is a promise."

CHAPTER SIX

CHARLOTTE WAS STILL numb sitting in an ornate bedroom in what looked like a fairy-tale castle hours later. The helicopter had landed in a clearing in a beautiful, orange-tinged forest, and left them there.

Then, as if summoned by the sheer force of Rafe's magnetism, a car had pulled up to the edge of the trees and driven them up the side of a mountain, up a winding dirt road that seemed chiseled into the side of it.

The castle was glorious, wreathed in gold, with dramatic turrets rising up and spiraling toward the sky. It seemed to be built straight from a rock face, or placed directly on top of the mountain.

At least there was a road. Otherwise, she would imagine it was impossible to escape this place.

Like it, and its inhabitants, had been trapped here by some kind of enchantment.

Of course, there seemed to be no town for miles. At least none she had seen when they had flown in, or when they had driven to the castle.

It was…it was profound isolation. And she had none of her own things with her. Only her purse, which at least contained her ID and her credit cards.

But, seeing as she felt as though she had been transported back in time, it didn't feel like any of those things would be useful to her.

She stood up, moving to an ornate vanity made from beautiful inlaid stones—jade, jasper and obsidian—and lined with gold. She looked at herself, stunned by the ridiculous contrast created by her reflection.

Her hair was escaping its confines, her face drawn and pale. Her black turtleneck sweater and blue jeans looked outrageously casual in her exceedingly formal surroundings.

Actually, she looked a little bit too casual for a kidnap victim, truth be told. She frowned. This was not the first time in her life she had been kidnapped. Charlotte had accepted a long time ago that her life wasn't normal. But this…well, this was just pushing the boundaries.

There was a knock on her door, and she made her way across the room, pulling it open just a crack and looking to see who was there. "Yes?" There was a woman there, one she had never seen before.

"Mr. Costa has requested that you come down to the study."

"I would like to request that Mr. Costa jump in a lake. Though, I imagine he wouldn't take terribly kindly to that."

The woman only looked at her blankly. Charlotte sighed heavily.

"I don't have a choice, do I?"

The woman shrugged. "I have a feeling that were you to refuse him, Mr. Costa would come up here and carry you down himself."

"That does sound like him." At least it sounded like the man he had become. A little bit too close to her father for Charlotte's liking. A man who was not opposed to keeping her locked away if he thought it would serve him. That made her chest feel like it was caving in on itself. It was even more painful than seeing him without his vision.

That change, the change that had clearly occurred in his soul, was much more disturbing than any physical change. A much greater loss, in her opinion.

Instead of arguing, she simply complied, leaving her bedroom and following the woman down the labyrinthine hallways. She reached up, brushing her fingertips against the wall, against the golden fleurs-de-lis that were stamped into the plaster.

This was what he had meant when he had talked about feeling the texture on the walls. About having a greater sense of the space than he did in a room composed of modern architecture. His home in London had more space, and she imagined that made things easier in some regards.

Nothing for him to trip over, everything set out

just so. But there was a richness here, a sense of place that she could not deny.

She would rather deny it. Because she would rather go ahead and just think he was crazy. That he was lost to her completely, and there was nothing of the man she cared for remaining.

Sadly, she didn't think that was the case. This was Rafe. The man, rather than the near boy she had known. He was successful. He was wealthy. She had read all about how power corrupted, and she had seen it firsthand over the course of her childhood.

She was only sorry to know that Rafe had not been immune.

She shook her head. She should have left him in the realm of fantasy. It would've been so much kinder to her poor heart. A heart that already felt so tender due to years of abuse and neglect.

She could have imagined Rafe forever as she wanted to think of him. But no. She had gone to find him. To have one blistering night with him, which had resulted in permanent consequences.

And him proving to be a controlling kidnapper.

The woman paused, then stepped to the side, opening up one of the ornate blue double doors, revealing a study, and Rafe, who was sitting in a wingback chair in front of the fireplace.

"Thank you," Charlotte said, turning to the woman, who had already vanished back into the gloom.

Charlotte sighed, then stepped into the study.

"Nice of you to join me," Rafe said.

Her heart began to speed up, then, as he looked in her direction, she felt it stall out completely. The way the flames highlighted his face was... intoxicating. Arresting.

His eyes looked black, fathomless. The stubble on his square jaw would be rough to the touch, as she already knew. And then there were his lips... Lips that she knew from experience would soften beneath her own, and then would get firm again as he assumed control. As he parted her lips and slipped his tongue into her mouth...

She felt her face heat, and she bit her cheek, doing her best to keep from making an idiot out of herself by betraying the fact that even now, when he had proven himself to be an undesirable louse, she still desired him.

"Well, much like my joining you here in this castle, I was left with very little choice."

"Still. It is very nice to put the veneer of civility over all of it, isn't it?"

"I'm not sure why you would care. It certainly isn't for my benefit. I don't have very much experience with civilized men. And you...you're no different. You're cut from the same cloth as my father, who thought nothing of physically moving me from one place to the other to do his bidding. Congratulations."

His face went hard as granite. "I am not like your father."

"Well, you could have fooled me. Dragging me off to a castle...intending to force me into marriage."

Rafe chuckled, pushing himself up from the armrests so that he was standing. He stepped to the side of the chair, held out his hand in front of the fire, then took a step closer, keeping his hand extended.

"I said nothing about marriage, *cara mia*."

She blinked, feeling incredibly stupid. Because he hadn't. "Well. As you're currently carrying me off like a marauder because I'm carrying your child—*children*—I assumed that you had designs on making them legitimate or something."

He shrugged, a casual and careless gesture. "I'm not legitimate. Why should I care if my children are?"

She didn't know what to say to that. Obviously, she had assumed that since he had kidnapped her, he wanted to keep her.

"This doesn't have anything to do with me, does it?"

She felt stupid. So stupid asking that question. And so very uncovered. Like he could see into her soul. See everything that she hoped way down at the bottom of her crushed heart. Because there were things she knew logically. Things she knew about him, about their situation, and about why it wasn't healthy in any way.

"This has everything to do with power," he said, his voice hard. It echoed what she had been thinking in the hallway. What she feared more than anything else.

That he wanted control. Whatever that might mean.

"And somehow, you had to take me back to a castle in order to feel like you had any? Honestly, Rafe, if I had not seen the contents of your underwear I would have thought that this had to do with some kind of inferiority complex."

He laughed at that, which surprised her. "You weren't going to tell me, were you?"

"I don't know," she answered honestly. "I really hadn't dealt with any of it mentally or emotionally. I still haven't."

"We do not know each other very well," he said, his dark brows locking together, lines appearing between them.

"I know you better than I know anyone else." She felt her face getting hot. "You have seen me naked, after all."

"You can see a great many women naked and never know them—on that you can trust me. You were certainly not the first woman I saw naked."

His lips tipped up, his smile rueful. "You were the last woman I saw naked, though."

Charlotte didn't know what to make of that statement. She wasn't clear on when his accident had happened in relation to their parting. But it must've been soon after. Because she couldn't imagine him pining for her after he had believed that she had...

"Rafe," she said. "Did you really think that I went off and married somebody else without giving you a thought? Did you really think that I was just amusing myself with you?"

"That's what rich people do," he said, his voice hard. "They use those without power as pawns in games that only they know the rules to."

"And you thought that I...you thought that I was doing that with you. That's really what you believed?"

"I didn't believe it. I didn't until I went to your room and was met by your stepmother. Clearly, she knew about us. Which meant your father did too."

"And she told you that I...that I betrayed you."

Pain gripped Charlotte by the throat, squeezing it tight. Of all the things she had imagined as
she had spent those years away from him. When
she had begun to see articles about his success,
it had never occurred to her that he had been led
to believe she had not only abandoned him but
had told her father about them.

She frowned, icy cold gripping her. "Rafe, how
did you escape? My father's not a forgiving man.
And we both knew...being together was risky. I
can't imagine that he would have let you..."

"He did not let me escape," Rafe said, his tone
dark. He turned away from the fire and began
to walk toward her. "The only reason I got away
from your father's estate alive is that he thought
he had killed me, and by the time he discovered
the truth...it was too late for him to do anything
about it. It was his intention that I leave in a body
bag. And in truth, I essentially did."

Rafe hadn't intended to tell Charlotte the story
so quickly. But then, there was no reason not
to. Here they were, holed up in this castle for

the foreseeable future. He intended to keep them both here until she was ready to give birth. He already had a doctor lined up, and he had paid her a very decent sum to attend to Charlotte and to look the other way if Charlotte were to mention that she was being held captive.

Oh, the power that came with money.

But power aside, they had time. And there was no reason to keep the story secret from her. It was true; the world did not know. But Charlotte might as well. She might as well understand exactly what had happened to him as a result of their assignation.

Yes, she had been in hiding for five years. Yes, it had certainly been difficult for her. But he had suffered greatly. He had lost greatly.

And then, she had been considering keeping his children from him. Another thing that would be stolen from him by the Adair family. He could not reconcile that. He could not endure it.

"When I climbed up to your room your stepmother was there on the balcony, waiting for me."

"Josefina is a serpent. She always has been."

"A bit of a cliché," he said drily. "The wicked stepmother."

"One I feel she took to heart."

"She told me you had gone. That you had confessed that I had been coming to your room at night, that you had elected to marry Stefan, who you felt was much more fitting of a woman in your position."

"How could you have believed her?" Charlotte asked, her voice torn with pain. "I told you that I would have given you everything. You wouldn't let me give it. I was not unwilling."

"Because I understood what you did not. That while you might have been willing at the time, you would come to resent me later. For all that you had left behind. For all that you had lost. I was never going to move you straight into similar circumstances, Charlotte, but you were too cosseted to think of such a thing. Because you could not imagine life without a tower."

"All I wanted was life outside the tower," she said. "You do me a disservice thinking otherwise."

"Then I did you a disservice. But it is in the past. And this conversation does not lead up to what you wanted to know. How did I escape?"

He heard her swallow, heard the rustle of fabric, and he wondered if that indicated she was fidgeting. He wasn't sure what she was wearing today, so he couldn't be certain of the way the fabric would sound when it moved.

"Tell me," she said. "I promise I won't interrupt again."

"I arrived, and there she was, standing on the balcony. She told me I was too late, and that you had gone. She also told me that your father was going to send guards, and that I would be dealt with. She said I would surely leave the property in a body bag. Her words. She was not wrong. She was smiling... It was very grotesque. She enjoyed my pain. Enjoyed threatening me. Somehow, I think your father had cast some blame on her for our tryst. Because she was the lady of the manor, I suppose, and hadn't realized I was sneaking into your room. She told me she wasn't going to allow me to destroy all she had built.

Would not allow us to be her downfall. I took a step away from her, and then I looked down over the balcony, and considered that I needed to climb back as quickly as possible and try to escape if I could. Because I knew she was correct. If your father's men found me, the only way I would leave was as a dead man. But while my focus was turned away...Josefina pushed me over the edge of the balcony. I was not paying attention, or there would have been no way she could have overpowered me. I was about to turn and climb down on my own, and she used that momentum against me."

He heard an indrawn gasp from Charlotte, a choked, distressed sound. "How did you survive that?"

"A true miracle and mystery," he said drily. "Though, the fact that I had my momentum broken by a couple of rocky ledges, and then again by the hedge that grows around the perimeter of the villa did help. Still. I sustained a severe head injury. And that swelling damaged my ability to see. For a while, they hoped that the swelling would go down, and that my vision would right itself. They say now that it is incredibly unlikely."

"But not impossible," Charlotte said.

"It does not benefit me to think of it as anything but impossible, Charlotte. I have never been one to hope for miracles. Everything I've ever gotten has come with bloodied knuckles and no small amount of struggle. My current status being no exception."

"Who helped you escape?" she asked.

"One of your father's men found me. Pietro. He was an older man who seemed...weary of the business. I had spoken with him a few times over the years. He used to talk about a woman he left behind when Michael called him in. He also owed your father a favor. He went to the estate, and he never returned home. He never saw the woman he loved again."

"That's sad."

"Life with your father was sad, as you well know. I think...I think he wished he could find his way back to something real again. To life. Love. He was sent down to the bottom of the

tower to collect my body, and to have me removed. But when he got down there he discovered that I was still breathing. Though most of
my bones were broken, and I was unconscious.
He took his life into his hands rescuing me. Covered me with a sheet and told your father that he
was off to dispose of me. Instead, he took me to
a local doctor that he said we could trust. That
man cared for me until I was stable. And then he
paid to have me moved to a hospital far away. I
was utterly dependent on strangers. My life was
in their hands. I despise being helpless. But a broken blind man who would be as good as dead if
his employer found out about his existence is as
helpless as it gets. I don't know what became of
Pietro when it was discovered that I was not in
fact dead. I imagine it didn't end well for him."
Rafe sighed heavily, thinking of that man and his
heavily lined face. One that relaxed only when
he spoke of his love. A love Rafe was certain
the man had never seen again. "I hope...I only
hope that he felt... He missed his humanity. He
told me that. I hope that whatever price he paid

in the end, he felt that what he did healed him in some way."

He heard her sit down, the heavy weight of her body as she plopped indelicately onto the settee he knew was positioned at about three o'clock.

"Rafe," she said softly. "I wish I would have known."

"Why?" He was truly curious about her rationale.

"Because I would have come to you. I would've come to find you. As it was I was off hiding. Hiding, and thinking only of myself. I had no reason to believe that you were in any trouble. I was told that you were fine. But you were off somewhere. And I didn't doubt it."

"So you would have come to find me, and then what? We would have been much easier to locate if both of us were in one place. And there would have been no way that I could have ever gone into the public eye if you and I were attached."

He wouldn't have cared. That much he knew. All those years ago, he would have taken the risk on her still.

But that would have been a mistake. Because his salvation had not come through Charlotte. It had come through money. It had come through power. Perhaps, the love of wealth truly was the root of all evil, but he would much rather that root be in his possession, something that he could grow and tend at will. Something that he could manipulate for his own ends.

He had been born powerless. And he had remained so until he had come into the position he was in now. It was irrefutable, undeniable.

"I just wish I would have known," she said. Silence hung between them, and he could hear her labored breathing. "I was very sorry. When I heard. And of course I did. When you became prominent, when you began to make the news, they said you were blind. And I knew it was because of some accident, which the media alluded to. But of course there were no details."

"There would be no details. Nobody knew what had befallen me. When I went to a hospital, I did not give them the real story. And so there was no way anyone could know. And unless your father purposefully chose to out himself and connect himself to me, there would be no way anyone could know."

"It was clever of you. Escaping him in that way. Because of that thin facade of respectability that he had. He would have known that he could not touch you. Not out in the open."

"He found it best to let it be. As it became clear that it was best if the both of us mutually did not acknowledge one another."

There was no sound then, nothing but the pop and hiss of the fire in the hearth. Then he heard her move, the faint slide of her fingers against skin, then through her hair.

It made him think of how that hair looked unbound. It made him ache. It made him want to shut out the outside world and take her in his arms again.

To erase the past.

But he couldn't go back. The sun was there. And he was here. Plunged into darkness.

"Money is the only real way to control your future, Charlotte," he said, his tone hard. "It is the leverage that is required to deal with difficult situations in life."

"True. Why would you talk to somebody when you can stick them in a helicopter and fly them up to a castle and detain them until you decide what to do with them?"

"You were not going to tell me about my child. I had no other choice. You don't understand. I have been manipulated too many times in my life, and I will not stand for it. Not again."

He heard her agitation. Her feet shuffling on the marble. Her abrupt shift in position. "How? How have you been manipulated?"

"I believe story time is over," he said, his voice hard.

"Fine." He heard the slap of her hands against fabric. "I can't understand you if you won't let me. I can't actually know you if you won't share with me what there is to know. You were just saying that we didn't know each other, but you're not allowing me to."

"It is unnecessary for the situation that we find ourselves in. We are not children playing at games of love anymore. We are having children that are going to come into a world where their father cannot see. I can leave nothing to chance. Not even you."

"So you're not going to trust me. You're not going to trust that I won't keep your children from you?"

"No," he said without hesitation.

"There is nothing I can do to change that?"

He gritted his teeth, so hard that they began to ache. "Charlotte, I trust no one but myself. That which I can manipulate with my own two hands. It has been proven to me that unless I seize control of something it will not be as I wish. It has been proven to me time and time again."

And with that, he walked out of the room. He knew the layout of this castle better than just about anything on earth. The map of the place inscribed upon his soul. It had been his mission upon purchasing it. To create a sizable domain that he could maneuver about with ease. And so, there were very specific instructions given to every member of staff. Everything was positioned just so. To the centimeter, exactly like the Braille map he had memorized when he had first purchased it.

Nothing was to be moved. Ever. And so it had been from the first. He spent a great amount of time here, and was more than able to conduct business from this location. Which was what he would continue to do until he came to a conclusion about exactly what he was to do with Charlotte. She had expected that he was going to force her into marriage of some kind, but he could see no benefit in that.

Marriage was simply a piece of paper. Easily walked away from. Easily destroyed. And Charlotte knew how to disappear. He needed something much more assuring.

Likely you could have gone with seduction if you had not kidnapped her.

He smiled ruefully at nothing and no one in particular. Yes, perhaps seduction would have been the better option. It said nothing good about him that he had gone to kidnapping first, he supposed. But it was too late.

That gave him pause.

Perhaps seduction was still the answer. Charlotte wanted trust. She wanted to feel as though she had some say in the situation. Wanted to feel as though she had some control. Charlotte wanted security and certainty. She wanted something of what they had once had.

He had lost that part of himself along with his sight, and it had never been an overly prominent part of him to begin with. She was the only person on the whole earth that he'd cared for in the way that he had. So, even then his faith in love had been somewhat tenuous.

It was gone altogether now, but that did not mean she had to believe so.

Control. That was the name of the game.

And what he had always found terribly inconvenient was that other people were so damned difficult to control. It was why he preferred his life stripped down to a series of transactions. Where there was him, and there was staff.

His dealings with Charlotte would require a different tactic.

But he was prepared for that. He had her exactly where he wanted. All he would have to do was maintain control of his own actions, and he would be able to obtain exactly what he wanted.

There were a great many things he found difficult these days. But control was not one of them.

CHAPTER SEVEN

CHARLOTTE WAS FEELING ANTSY. After her conversation with Rafe the night before she had gone to bed and slept fitfully. Then she had woken with her mouth tasting like the inside of an old fast-food wrapper, and her body feeling like it had been run over by a car. Her head hurt, and her entire being just felt stale. It was difficult to know what to do now. Difficult to know what the best course of action was.

It was terribly isolating, being in this castle. Not that she wasn't used to isolation. It was just that this was outside her control. And for the past five years her isolation had been self-imposed.

She had decided when she would move; she had decided where she would live and where she would work. All her interactions with her friends had been carefully planned, of course.

But she was supposed to be done with that, and Rafe had come in and uprooted her. Plus, she was having his babies.

All of that had been lost somehow. Probably in the kidnapping. It was very difficult to maintain one's wits when one was whisked to a castle in a helicopter against one's will.

She was having twins.

Her heart clenched tight, and so did her stomach.

She made a dash to the restroom, just in time to lose what little she had eaten the night before. She emerged again feeling clammy and unsteady.

She dressed slowly in the clothes she had been wearing the day before. Last night before bed a member of staff had provided her with a pair of pajamas, but there was still nothing else. She had been informed that a new wardrobe would be coming soon. But as concerns went, it was on the bottom of the list. She sighed heavily, looking at her reflection in the mirror again, which was yet more waxen and disheveled than it had been yesterday.

She opened up the door to her bedroom and saw a tray laden with breakfast sitting outside. She wrinkled her nose, then stepped over it. She wanted nothing to do with food. Not at the moment.

She walked down the circular staircase, and found herself standing in a large antechamber. She thought it was perhaps at the front of the castle. But she found the whole thing mazelike and disorienting. She couldn't fathom how Rafe navigated it. She had a hard enough time using all of her senses, and he was deprived of one of his and seemed to have no trouble getting around.

But then, as with all things, Rafe liked to maintain control. Which meant getting around the palace wasn't difficult. That much she could surmise from just knowing him.

Her heart twisted. The way he had talked about being dependent on other people after his accident...

What a horrible thing. For a man like him, feeling powerless, feeling helpless. It truly was one of the worst imaginable fates. Aside from death.

His very survival had depended on the kindness of others.

Even given her present circumstance, she could feel bad for him about that.

She inhaled the scent of the air, and she yet again understood exactly what he meant when he spoke of the atmosphere in the palace versus modern architecture. It was different. You could smell the age and the walls, not unpleasant, but certainly unmistakable. It was clean, but this was not something that would get wiped away.

Right now, it was all a bit overpowering to her. Her senses had become notably enhanced over the past week or so, and at the moment smells were an assault.

She moved through the antechamber, and down a corridor, and that led to a room that was made entirely of windows. The light was so bright here, pouring in from outside like buckets of gold, bringing both warmth and a sense of space to the room.

That was when she noticed that toward the back of the room, the two panels in the middle weren't windows at all, but doors.

That was what she needed. To get outside. To clear her head.

She began to walk across the room when the same woman from last night came in. "Miss," the woman said. "Mr. Costa is looking for you."

Of course. The master desired her presence, and therefore she was fetched and expected to comply. She was not in the mood.

"Then Mr. Costa will simply have to keep looking for a while," she said, feeling stubborn, a little bit nauseous and really not in the mood.

"Miss, I don't think that is a good idea."

"If Mr. Costa would like to speak to me, he can come out to the garden."

The woman looked ashen at the very idea of someone defying Mr. Costa. "Mr. Costa does not come out to the garden."

But Charlotte was resolute. "Then Mr. Costa will have to wait."

She walked with a purposeful stride to the doors, then wrenched the first one open. She could tell that it hadn't been used in a long while. Again, not her concern.

Rafe had spirited her away to his castle out in

the middle of Germany, and it was not her job to be a compliant captive. She had done so long enough. And while she was grieved to discover that Rafe was more like her father than he had once been, she knew that he wasn't going to throw her off the top of the castle for insubordination.

She stepped outside, closing the door behind her, allowing the chill autumn air to wash over her.

It was a garden, but it certainly wasn't kept up. Everything was overgrown, in a state of disarray. There were great stone statues with vines growing up around them, making everything look as though nature was trying to reclaim it, drag it back down into the earth and render it to dust again.

She breathed out, her breath lingering on a cloud. It was so quiet here. The only sound was the occasional rustle of the leaves overhead, a few birds flitting here and there, chirping to their mates.

She had often found solace in nature. Actually, this moment reminded her of when she had first escaped into the woods after her father's men had taken her captive. They had not imagined that she would run to the woods. Because they had thought her too cosseted. What they had not understood was that it was the only thing that kept her sane all that time she'd been captive in her own home.

Walks on the estate, where she didn't feel so much like she was under the watchful gaze of her father.

She kept on walking down the little path that was well overgrown, until she found a stone bench. Then she sat down, closing her eyes and letting the breeze ruffle her hair, which was up in its usual bun.

She hadn't had a chance to do anything else with it yet. To cut it off.

She had fully intended to after her night with Rafe. And then she just…hadn't. There had been other things. The will, and making sure her apartment was in order. Hair had been a low priority. Then she had started feeling unwell. And after that, it had become clear that she needed to do some research on that unwellness.

And then there had been the pregnancy tests. And the doctor. And Rafe. It seemed to always come back to Rafe.

She let her eyes flutter closed, and she felt exhaustion sweep over her. Even though she had just woken up, she was feeling unaccountably run down. Pregnancy was hard.

And now she felt like her head was swimming. Just thinking about pregnancy. About the fact that it meant there would be a baby... No, two babies.

She laid her head down against the bench, the cool stone a vague comfort as anxiety overtook her. She just needed to rest. Just for a moment. And then maybe everything would be slightly clearer.

"Where is she?" he asked, addressing Della, his housekeeper.

"She went outside hours ago," Della said. "No one has seen her since."

Rage spiked through him. She had defied him earlier, and he had allowed it in the interest of being less of a tyrant to her. He wanted to seduce her after all. To forge a bond between them. For there he would find true control.

Overtly raging at her over every defiance would not accomplish that.

But this...he could not allow this.

"And you did not think to come and tell me before this?"

"Forgive me, Mr. Costa," she said, her voice sounding not in the least bit contrite. "I was not clear as to whether or not our guest was in fact a prisoner. It did not occur to me that she could not make her way around the grounds if she did not wish to remain inside."

"She is a flight risk," he said, his voice hard. "And she is carrying my children. Therefore, her safety and her whereabouts are of the utmost importance to me."

Della let out a small, shocked sound. That, at least, he found satisfying. At least something rattled her.

"She went out to the garden?"

"Yes, sir."

He could easily send a member of his staff out there. But it was not what he wished. Because she was defying him, openly. She would have to learn that he did not bring her here to play games.

He attempted to remind himself of his earlier conclusion. That he needed to tread lightly with her. That he needed to try to seduce her—emotionally and physically. But it was lost somewhere in his rage.

He had brought her to this place that he knew better than anywhere else, and she had taken herself off to the portion of it that he did not frequent.

He made his way to the solarium, and across to where he knew the doors were. The third and fourth panel down from the end of the room. He pressed his hand against it, made certain that it was in fact the exit, and then walked through it into the outside. He listened. But he heard nothing. Not any sound of movement at all. Just the wind in the trees.

She could not have run away. There was no way. It would be an impossible walk to civilization, and he was under the impression she was suffering from morning sickness.

Of course, *she* didn't know how far the nearest town was. That was part of the problem. She wasn't familiar with this place. And when she had run from her father...

He curled his hands into fists, uncomfortable with that thought. That he could possibly compare her running away from her father, running away from her forced marriage, to this.

He wasn't going to force her into anything.

No, you're simply going to manipulate her into it.

He scowled, and then continued to walk across the dilapidated garden. He swept the ground with his cane, making sure that he wasn't surprised by any uneven terrain. His cane struck something hard that protruded from the ground. A rock or brick in an unkempt path perhaps.

He could call her name. And perhaps, she would answer. But that would only work if she wasn't actually hiding from him. And he suspected that she was. More than *suspected*, he was *certain* that she was. Anger and a sense of helplessness washed over him. He hated this. Hated feeling like he couldn't tackle something on his own, but he was starting to think that he was going to have to walk back to the house and ask for assistance.

Fortunately, he had a strong sense of direction, where he had come from. That was imperative in his situation.

He stopped for a moment, taking stock of the direction the breeze was blowing. He tilted his head upward, a gold circle appearing on his vision. The sun. He could sense changes in light.

It was helpful. Of course, as Charlotte was not charting any kind of natural course, it was of no help to him. Charlotte was simply being difficult.

He continued walking down the path, and then his cane hit something hard. He swept it up, got the impression of a long slab of something—most likely stone—with another slab laid over the top. A bench. That was the most likely item.

"Be careful!" Someone grabbed hold of the

end of his cane. And he recognized Charlotte's grumpy voice instantly.

"Charlotte?"

He heard shifting, and then the rustle of leaves. "I fell asleep. How did you...how did you find me?"

He was so relieved to find her here his knees nearly buckled. So relieved she wasn't out wandering the forest. Pregnant. Alone.

"I tracked you using only your scent," he said, his tone dry. "You know, when one loses their sight their other senses are heightened."

"I don't believe that."

He lifted a shoulder. "It's true."

"No, I believe your other senses are heightened, but I don't believe you tracked me like a bloodhound." He heard a small, shuffling sound and a little snort and he thought she was probably scrubbing her face. He wanted to laugh because the image it created was a cute one; he couldn't deny it. "I don't smell," she protested further.

He begged to differ with her there. She did smell. It was exactly how he had recognized her the first time he had seen her. That sweet floral scent that he had only ever associated with her.

"If you say so."

"I just needed some time outside the house."

"Charlotte, you cannot leave the castle."

"I'm sorry, Rafe, but I will leave the castle if I choose to. I can't be kept captive in there."

"Yes, you can. Because you have no idea where you are out here."

There was a pause. "No, I think you have no idea where you are out here," she said, far too astute for his liking.

"I found my way just fine."

"But you don't *know* it. You don't know this whole terrain. And you don't like that."

"Charlotte..."

"I am not a *thing* that you can manipulate at will, Rafe Costa. I never have been. I don't understand how you can do this to me knowing what my father did."

The wind kicked up again, the scent of damp leaves and low-hanging clouds on the air. "I'm not your father."

"You're treading dangerously close to being cut from the same cloth."

"Except were I your father, I would be fashioning some way to punish you grandly for your insubordination. He enjoyed that. Punishing people."

She laughed, a kind of crystalline sound that sounded easily broken. And if it did break, he had a feeling it could cut them both.

"You don't think I know that?" Her voice trembled. "Of course, he didn't ever physically harm me. I was a bargaining tool, and he didn't want to damage my beauty. But he kept so much from me. The outside world. He did his best to make sure that were I ever to try to go out in it, I would be hobbled. Unable to function without his say-so. I'm well aware of the kind of mental torture my father was capable of putting people under."

"Physical torture, as well," Rafe said, his tone grave. He wasn't in the mood to play nice with her. Moreover, he wasn't in the mood to be sensitive about her feelings. Despite what she might feel, he was not her father, and she would do well to remember it.

"He had people hired specifically to torture anyone who went against him. To break bones."

There was a long beat of silence. "Did you ever do that?"

"No," he said simply. "But I saw it."

He heard leaves rustling. Charlotte fidgeting. Choosing her next words with care, he imagined. "This is what I don't understand, Rafe. Why didn't you stop any of this? Why were you with him at all?"

Much like the story of his blindness, there was no reason to keep this from her either. "I was forced into it. As I said, money is power. Your father saved me from being put in prison back in Rome when I was caught stealing. Not only did he do that—he offered me an education. He paid for my mother to have housing. We had been homeless for a long time by that point."

"If it were any other man, then I would say that was quite generous of him. But not with my father."

"He was only buying a sycophant," Rafe said, "and he knew that once he held my mother's fate in his hands, he had a great deal of power over me."

"What happened to your mother after you…"

"That's the thing. Once he thought I was dead, he had forgotten that he was paying to put my mother up. When he was no longer using her for leverage, there was no reason for him to throw her out onto the street just for fun. If there was no one around to be hurt by her demise, he didn't have a taste for it. Or he didn't have a thought about it. And, once I gained my own position of power, I installed her in a home where she very happily lives now."

"Do you see her?"

He laughed, hard and bitter. "No. I have no desire to. She only asks for more money, and while I do not begrudge her a certain amount…"

"You never spoke of her. When we were together. You never told me about your mother."

"There are a great many things I never told you about."

"Yes," Charlotte said. "And I wonder why. You risked yourself to be with me... But then, it makes me wonder if you really did? If you assumed that we were doomed, I suppose it was much easier to play at love. Much simpler."

"I am not playing games with you now," he said, her words striking him somewhere unsettling. "I will not be denied my children, Charlotte. I will not allow you to dictate the terms here." He made an attempt to soften his tone. "You could be happy here. With me."

"If that were true, don't you suppose I would have been happy in the tower that my father made too?"

CHAPTER EIGHT

RAFE SUCCESSFULLY AVOIDED her for the next week. Or maybe he wasn't avoiding her; that was always a possibility.

But she doubted it.

He was far too much in control for anything to be accidental. If Rafe had wanted to see her, then she would have seen him. For the man left absolutely nothing to chance, and there was nothing that he did not manipulate in his domain.

She sighed heavily, pacing back and forth in the solarium, which she had come to think of as her room. She did still go out to the gardens, in spite of the discussion that he'd had with her last week. He might have taken her hostage, but he was not going to dictate what she did with her time in her gilded little cage.

There was nowhere for her to run, after all, and she was not going to forgo fresh air.

Today, though, it was raining, and she was taking advantage of what weak, pale sunlight was coming through the windows.

She grabbed hold of one of the settees and pushed it across the highly polished marble floor, positioning it in front of the window. Then she got the side table and did the same with that. It was much nicer with everything right by the window. For a while, she just wanted to sit and gaze out at the view; she wasn't in the mood to go and brave Rafe.

After a while she decided that it would be better if she had a cup of tea. She could ask one of Rafe's staff members to get it for her. They were very attentive, and she often got the feeling that Della—his head of staff—disapproved of his keeping her here.

It made her feel...if not safe, then at least as though she had an ally. It was nice to have an ally.

Not that Della could do anything about it either. She needed the job, presumably. And going against Rafe would mean the loss of a job. He did not run a democracy. This was a dictatorship— no doubt about it.

But Charlotte was feeling surprisingly good today, and she didn't want anyone to wait on her. She wanted to get tea by her own power. She just needed to do something.

That was the problem with being cooped up in this place. It reminded her too much of the past. And it gave her far too much time to think.

There was a lot of brooding, of course. A lot of unhappiness about what Rafe had become. But then, inevitably, it led to memories of their time together. Bittersweet and painful feelings. How he had made her feel cared for, loved, for the first time in her memory.

And that was why it was so difficult to hate him now. Why it was hard not to hope whenever she heard footsteps that it was Rafe coming into the room to see her.

Because he was the one who had taught her what it meant to be cared for. And perhaps it had all faded, broken apart in the ensuing years.

The lies from Josefina, the damage done in his injury and the time apart were all too much for that fledgling love to survive.

It was as if they'd gone through a cold winter. A deep freeze. And that tender blossom had been killed.

But nonetheless, she remembered it. As if it were the only flower she had ever seen.

He was her only reference for it. And that made it...

She couldn't hate him. Even if she should.

She wandered into the kitchen, found a pot of boiling water on the stove and set about making herself a cup of tea.

When she arrived back at the solarium, she walked in to see Rafe, making his way across the room, and she saw the accident without enough time to prevent it. He charged straight through the center of the room near the windows, and then went over the end table that she had placed just by the settee, his knee going straight through the top of the thin wood as he, and the furniture, crashed down to the marble floor.

Charlotte's heart leaped up into her throat, and she released her hold on her cup of tea, the porcelain shattering on the ground, her penance, in some ways for what had just happened. For the broken table. That she needed to break something too. So that he wasn't alone.

It didn't make sense; she knew it. But then, she didn't have sense in her head right now. She had feeling. And nothing more.

Regret. Anguish. That she had cost him his pride just now. And that he might be hurt.

He was swearing in Italian, the words sharp and vile, even if she couldn't understand them all. The intent was clear. And she was frozen.

Then he extricated himself from the table, his dress pants torn, the skin beneath bloodied. He had obviously hit his forehead on something; a dark red circle was forming there.

"I am so sorry," she said, her voice trembling.

"Did you move this?" His voice was terrifyingly cold. Arctic.

She nodded, then realized he couldn't see. And she almost broke. Just like the teacup. "I wasn't thinking. I moved it so that I could sit closer to the window, and then I went into the kitchen to get a cup of tea. I didn't think about you walking in. We haven't crossed paths in a week. I thought the odds of you coming into the room where I was would be unlikely."

That wasn't true. She hadn't thought at all. Hadn't thought that of course it would be dangerous to move something out of one of his well-worn paths.

Of course Rafe knew the castle. If he didn't, he would not be able to navigate it as he did. Most of the time she had seen him wandering the halls, it had been without his cane even. So she had to assume that to a degree, he had muscle memory associated with the place. And of course that meant things couldn't simply be moved from their spots.

"That isn't true," she said. "I was thoughtless. I'm sorry."

He crossed the room in her direction, following the sound of her voice. And she froze. He looked like a madman, enraged, almost out of his mind with it. His dark eyes were wild, fixed on nothing. His lip curled into a sneer.

"Rafe..."

He reached out, wrapping his arm around her waist and hauling her up against him. Then he gripped hold of her chin with his thumb and forefinger, holding her steady for a moment. He held her like that for one heartbeat. Two.

Then his fingertips began to drift down the side of her neck, and he curved them around her throat, pressing his thumb against the place where her pulse was beating rapidly.

"Are you afraid of me?" he rasped.

"I'm afraid *for* you," she said, her voice trembling.

"There is no need to be afraid for me, *cara*. But if you truly think that I am like your father, then perhaps, fear of me is the reason that your heart should be racing so fast."

"You're not my father."

"You must never move things in my home. This is not your domain. This is mine. We are not sharing this. It is not a happy household. You do not have free rein of it. You cannot go where you wish. You cannot touch just anything. It is not up to you to decide what goes where. This is *mine*. Mine alone."

She lifted a trembling hand, touched the side of his cheek, then reached up to his forehead, trying to soothe the angry red welt there. "I'm sorry," she whispered.

CHAPTER NINE

RAFE'S BLOOD WAS PUMPING, his pride burning more than anything else. He despised this. Despised how easily it was for him to be made to look like a fool. A bumbling idiot in his own home. How dependent he was on others doing exactly as he bade them. How remarkably like a child he felt at times. It was as appalling as it was enraging.

And she was *sorry*.

His blood was running hot. Rage over his injury. Desire from her nearness. That intoxicating scent that was only Charlotte.

"If you want to show me how sorry you are, perhaps it would be best for you to start on your knees." The words were hard-edged and cruel, and he expected very much for her to slap him across the face.

Except she did not slap him. She continued to touch him as though he were a fragile thing and she was attempting to make sure he had not been cracked or dented.

For God's sake, he had been thrown from a tower and he had not allowed it to break him. This indignity—witnessed by one small woman—would not leave him reduced.

He wrapped his fingers around her wrist, holding her like an iron manacle. Stopping her from stroking him as if he were a puppy.

"I will not be placated," he said. "Do you want to make up for your transgression, or not?"

She was trembling now, and he didn't know if it was from fear or from something else. He wasn't sure if he cared.

"You know I'm attracted to you," she said, her voice thick. "But is this how you want it? You want to demand it? In anger?"

"Yes. This is how I want it. You can always leave if this disturbs you. Otherwise, I suggest you apologize to me using that lush mouth of yours, and no words."

He expected her to run then. Expected her to flee his wrath.

Instead, she began to lower herself before him. He curved his hand around to her hair, and almost as if on a reflex he pulled the pin from her long, silky locks.

"Don't," she said. "I will keep that for myself."

He lowered his hand then, not trusting himself to comply with her wishes if he did not. And why the hell *should* he? He was the one who was injured. He was the one who had been made a mockery of in his own home.

He was not the one who should feel guilty. She should feel guilty. She should feel full of contrition. She ought to be lowering herself in front of him. It was no less than he deserved.

And yet, no matter how forcefully he spoke those words in his mind, he did not believe them.

She did not touch his belt. Did not touch his zipper. Instead, he felt the thin fabric of his pants, being swept aside where they were torn at the knee.

"You're bleeding," she said softly.

She leaned in, blowing cool breath onto the wound, the sensation both soothing and arousing.

"I know," he responded, the words hard.

"You're bleeding, and it's my fault." Her words were choked. "And I understand why you think you need to make me bleed too."

"I don't want your blood," he spat, the words savage. "I want your mouth. On me."

"And I have no problem giving you that. But I suppose that robs you of something. I suppose that takes away the punishment."

But she didn't move. Instead, she continued to blow on his knee, as though he were a child and she was soothing him as if he were having a tantrum after an injury.

But then, then she moved. Letting her hand slide up his thigh and inward, cupping his arousal, moving her palm along his hardened length.

"You're angry at me, but you still want me," she said. "How's that for control?"

"I did not ask for a commentary," he bit out.

"No, certainly not," she murmured.

"Your mouth should be busy."

He felt her shift, move up higher as she undid his belt, then undid the closure of his slacks. He heard her breath hiss through her teeth as she took his erection into her hand.

He would give an inestimable amount of his fortune in that moment to be able to look down and see the way that she appeared then. Her blond hair wound into a tight coil of spun gold, her cheeks undoubtedly flushed from anger if not from arousal. And once she started to work on his arousal, her lips becoming slick and red. Swollen.

Just the idea made him jump in her hand.

She tested him with the tip of her tongue, the movement slow and slick and tantalizing, a lush glide into madness. And then the heat of her mouth engulfed him as she took him deep. As she gave an apology with her lips, her tongue and the controlled edge of her teeth. She gripped him firmly as she worked him just the way he had taught her all those years ago. She had not forgotten.

And he knew there had been no other men.

She had come to his bed a virgin, just as he had left her.

Waiting for him. *Waiting for him.*

It didn't matter if it wasn't true. It was the war cry that raged through his blood as Charlotte pleasured him. As his whole world broke apart and fireworks flashed in his mind, his entire being lighting up even while his vision remained dark.

He spent himself. Pleasure a feral creature inside him tearing at his gut, dragging him down into an abyss that he could find no way out of. An abyss he wanted to stay in.

And then, there was nothing but sound of their fractured breathing in the empty room, and he could think of nothing but the picture it must present. Charlotte on her knees before him, a broken cup—he presumed—on the floor nearby. Splintered furniture. And him standing there with torn dress pants and a bloodied knee.

He was supposed to be seducing her. Seducing her body. Seducing her heart. And what had he done? He had growled at her like a bear and then forced her to give him pleasure at the first sign things were not going according to his plan. He had avoided her for the past week, and then at first contact he had done this.

He had no control with her. He had made a plan, but he could not seem to stick to it, and that was untenable. Incomprehensible.

And so he bent down and swept her up from the ground, holding her close to his chest.

"Rafe..."

"Is there anything else you've moved?"

"No..."

He swept through the solarium, back toward the quarters of the house where nothing had been touched. And at last he felt powerful again. At last he felt like the master.

Carrying Charlotte. Like she was weak and he was strong. She was clinging to him, her arms around his neck, her body frozen. Probably in fear.

Probably deserved.

He had to fix this. One way or another. He had to find a way to make it so she would stay with him.

She was carrying his children, after all, and it was imperative.

He would not become his father.

Never.

He moved quickly down the corridor, then up a curved staircase, counting each stair in his head as he went, nearly unconscious exercise, and then finished perfectly, expectedly, before carrying her down another long corridor toward his chamber.

He pushed the door open, took them across the threshold and then deposited her at the foot of his bed.

"Do you see why things must never move?"

"I see," she said, her voice sounding thin.

Something in him hurt, a sharp pain in his chest that outdid the one in his knee and forehead. "I didn't hurt you, did I?"

He found that he actually cared what the answer was. Found that it actually would bother him if he had harmed her in some way.

"I'm fine," she said, still sounding somewhat dazed.

"This distance between us cannot be," he said, his voice rough.

This was only part of his plan. He had to repair now what he had broken, and clearly he could not be trusted to do it by interacting with her. Clearly, if they spoke, he was going to destroy it. He did not know how to say the right things. But he could pleasure her. That much he knew he could do.

He did not need to see to know the map of the castle. And just the same, he did not need to see in order to know the map of Charlotte's body. It was burned into his mind. The last woman he had ever seen naked. He would remember her always, and even if he had seen a thousand women after her he would imagine that would be the case.

"And what underwear do you have on today?" he asked.

"They're quite plain," she said.

"A pity. But then, you won't mind taking them off for me."

"Did I say that I would take them off for you?" He supposed he deserved that.

"Will you?" A request, which was painful, but necessary at this point.

There was a slight hesitation. "Why?"

"So that we can...so that we... I'm the one who's blind," he said. "I should think that you would be able to see quite clearly exactly what my body wants." Unfamiliar shame lashed at him.

"You want to have sex with me, but I want to know why. Is it to satisfy yourself, or do you want something else? Because I have been a weapon for men for a very long time, Rafe, and I would like this to be about something else. Something more than manipulation. Something more than just satisfying you."

He would be a liar if he told her it wasn't about manipulation. But then, he had never fancied himself a man of great integrity. What did it matter? What did it matter if it was what she wanted to hear? If it would make her happy with him? Selfless reasons, after all.

"What I did downstairs," he said, "that was selfish. That was for my own pleasure, and more than that, for my ego. Because falling like that is never easy for a man like me. But now, now that I am seeing clearer…"

"Orgasm does that for you, does it?"

"Perhaps," he responded drily. "Nonetheless, I want to pleasure you now. To give you a gift, as you just gave to me."

"Your knee looks terrible. You'll hurt yourself."

"I don't care."

He lifted her up against him, wrapped her legs around his waist and then lowered them both to the bed. The brocade of the comforter rubbed into his wound, and he gritted his teeth, hating to acknowledge that she was right.

"I told you," she said softly, touching his face, and then tracing a path down his chin, down his neck, her fingertips landing at the base of his throat. "Your heart is beating fast," she said.

"Because I want you," he said.

He reversed their positions, bringing her to a seated pose over the top of him, so that she was astride him. "If you're so concerned for my knee, you can always do it this way."

He heard rustling, and he knew she had taken off her shirt. Then her bra. He put his hands on her hips, felt the waistband of her jeans and where it bordered soft skin.

"Quite casual attire for a palace," he remarked.

"Yes, well. Some dresses were purchased for me, but today it's awfully cold."

"I should like you to wear a dress for me."

"Would you?" He heard a smile in her voice.

"Yes. Because I should like very much to remove one from your body again. To push a skirt up over your hips and take you that way."

"I didn't realize this had become a standing arrangement."

"I didn't realize that you talked so much."

She huffed out a laugh. "I feel I should be offended by that."

"But you aren't. Because you're too turned on. You want me too much to be angry with me."

"You're very arrogant," she said, but she wiggled her hips in a way that let him know he was correct.

"Yes," he responded. "Very arrogant. But at

this point in my life would you like my ego to be any more wounded than it already has been?"

She pressed a quick kiss to the corner of his mouth. "No."

She pressed a firm hand to the center of his chest, then braced herself as she lifted up away from him. She wiggled, and he figured that she was trying to get out of her jeans. So he thought he would make himself useful.

He gripped her hips with both hands, then took hold of the waistband of her jeans, lifting her slightly as he pulled them down her thighs. She squeaked, then began kicking them the rest of the way off.

Then she took her position back over the top of him. She began to work his shirt, pulling it from his body, then shoving his pants down the rest of the way. Leaving them both naked.

He slid his hands up from her hips, letting them glide over the indent to her waist, and up farther to her breasts. He skimmed his thumbs over her tightened nipples, then tested their weight in his hands.

Visions of pale skin, curved lines and silk bled through the black in his mind. Bright pops on dark velvet, laced through with the sounds of her bliss. And somehow he could envision it all.

She gasped, a sound of sweet benediction that he let wash over him like a baptism. He felt new. In this moment. Didn't feel quite so stained by the past. By the anger that had consumed him in the solarium. By the anger that had consumed him for years.

He moved his hands back down to her hips, tilted her forward slightly and settled her over the head of his aching arousal. She gasped, rocked herself forward experimentally, then back again, taking part of him in, then settling herself down, inch by excruciating inch.

She pressed her forehead against his, her breath warm against his lips as she shuddered, rolling her hips, pleasure like a lightning strike that started at the base of his spine and shot upward. She was electric. And he could only absorb that energy.

Then he lost control. Lost the ability to simply

lay there, at the mercy of her electrical storm. He gripped her hips, bucking upward, bringing her down hard onto him. She gasped, then sobbed, grabbing hold of his shoulders, her fingernails digging into his flesh.

Pleasure and pain wrapped themselves around his mind, a bold red slash he could visualize, cutting down through his soul.

"Tell me," he ground out. "Tell me you want this. Tell me it's good."

"It is," she moaned.

He would give anything to see the desire written across her face. To see how it looked when her lips parted as she sounded her pleasure.

But he shut that down. Because it was no use wanting that. No use thinking about it. Instead, he focused on the feel of her skin beneath his hands. The way those soft hips gave beneath his touch. The sounds she made when she breathed. The way her breath increased when he did something she liked particularly. The soft hitch in the back of her throat.

And he could smell her. Sex, desire, mixed together with flowers and Charlotte. He was lost in that. In the way all of his senses lit up when he was with her like this. He could feel. Deeply. Exquisitely. That slick glide of her body around his erection. The way the pads of her fingertips felt on his skin, and the little half-moon fingernails digging in. He imagined she was leaving marks behind. He would never see them with his eyes. But he could feel the shape of them. The depth. Could see it in his mind as a color. Could hear, somehow. The sound of her indrawn breath. A gasp of need.

He reached between them, slid his fingertips along her inner thigh until she shook. Until he found the sensitive notch of flesh at the apex of her thighs and rubbed in a circular motion until he felt her begin to pulse around him. Until he felt her release hold on her control and give in to the powerful orgasm that shook her entire body.

But he wasn't done. Not even close.

He'd come once already. He would not leave this unequal.

He reversed their positions, uncaring now about

the way the brocade bedding bit into his wound. It only added to all this. It felt like a knife. Tasted like metal. More feelings. More.

He craved it all.

Rafe pulled back, then rocked forward slowly, tormenting them both with long, slow strokes.

He lowered his head, nuzzled her neck, just beneath her chin, and down to her breasts. Then he took one sweet nipple into his mouth, sucked hard, before turning his attention to the other one.

She was everything beautiful. Ripe and luscious, and all that he wanted. All that he needed.

Light danced across the darkness of his vision, streaks of heat pouring down over his veins. She made him see light. More than that, she made him feel it. All the way down into his soul. Touching the darkness that went deeper than blindness.

And after that, he had no control left. He needed her to come again. Needed to do something to make amends for what had happened earlier. But he couldn't hold back. Not anymore.

"Come for me," he said, the words fractured.

"Please," he said, begging now, and he didn't even care.

He felt her arch beneath him, her entire body going stiff as she cried out, her second release like a raging storm, catching him up in the tide, consuming them both. His own orgasm was torn from him, as painful as it was pleasurable. And when it was over, he felt like he had lost something vital of himself, and replaced it with something just as essential. He had no idea what that feeling could possibly be. That intense feeling of loss, of surrender, coupled with a satisfaction like he had never known.

She curled up against him, a warm, soft weight of her body playing havoc with him. With his sense of time and space. He knew that it was early in the day. And yet he very much wanted to stay in bed. Very much wanted to allow the post-sex lethargy to carry him under. To hold her against him.

To embrace the darkness that surrounded him, always, and allow it to create a kind of intimacy between them. A closeness. To allow her to steal the careful control he exerted over his world. If only for a few hours.

His routine had become very important to him over the past few years. To train his internal clock so that he didn't make mistakes about when he went to bed, and when he woke up. He was dependent upon alarms and timers, but he also had worked very hard to instill the feeling of time into himself.

He didn't care right now. He cared about nothing but the way she felt, draped over him, pressed against him.

And so, he let himself drift off to sleep.

When Charlotte woke it was late in the afternoon. She was surprised that she had slept for so long. And even more surprised that Rafe was asleep by her side.

Carefully, she slipped out from beneath the covers, quietly moving to collect her clothes. She felt raw. Raw and fragile, and she needed to go away to clear her head. She knew that, given the circumstances of what had occurred between them earlier, her hiding from him might not be received very well.

If he sent someone after her, she would go speak to him. She just needed a little bit of time. She needed…something.

"To not fall in love with him?" She whispered those words to herself after she closed the door to his bedroom behind her and began to walk as silently as possible down the corridor.

Yes, she would really appreciate not falling in love with him. Not again. Because Rafe—as he was now—did not seem to be the kind of man who understood love.

The way he had behaved with her in the solarium…

She should be angry. But then, in order to be angry she'd have to convince herself she had been forced. And she had made her choice. He had given her the chance to turn away, but she had wanted to meet his challenge head-on. Had been determined that she would get her own back by stealing his opportunity to punish her. By proving to him just how much she wanted him.

And then…then they had gone to his bedroom. And what had happened there had been nothing short of soul shattering.

Rafe wanted control. And honestly, she could understand. She wanted some too. Which put them dangerously at odds, since he seemed to think that in order to control any aspect of this he had to control her entirely.

She went back into the solarium and saw the mess had been cleaned up. Saw that the couch had been moved back to the position it was in before she had foolishly adjusted it.

And she stood there, realization of what she had done—not earlier, but just now when she had left his room—washing over her.

She looked around, hoping that she could find a member of staff. She walked outside the solarium, toward the kitchen, where she saw Della.

"Della," she said. "Do you have a first-aid kit?"

"Yes," the older woman said.

"I need one. For Mr. Costa. He was injured earlier. Because I was an idiot and I moved the furniture."

"I'll get you one. Would you like me to see to him?"

Charlotte shook her head. "No. I think that I should."

"For the record," the housekeeper said, "I think it is good for Mr. Costa to not have everything go his way."

"I think he's had quite enough not go his way," Charlotte said, her heart clenching.

Della shrugged. "In some ways. But not in all ways. Wait here."

CHAPTER TEN

WHEN RAFE WOKE, he was disoriented, and there were cool, delicate hands against his skin.

"What…"

"I'm bandaging your leg." Charlotte, of course. His body had recognized her before she'd even spoken to him. "Don't be difficult."

"Why did you assume that I would be difficult?"

"Because difficult is your only setting as far as I can see, Rafe Costa." He felt something sticky and cold against his skin. It had to be medicine. She was tending him. He wanted to be angry. Angry that she was treating him like this again.

But she was touching him. And he could not find it in him to be enraged when she was touching him.

"You have to be at least as hard as life, don't you think?"

"No," she answered. "I don't think."

"And why do you disagree with me?"

"Because. That just makes me think of banging two rocks together."

He laughed, then winced as she added yet more medicine to his knee. "That is how you get a spark, is it not?"

"Sure. But what's the point of it? I mean, in the end, all you're doing is sitting there banging two hard things together. There's no nuance in that. There certainly isn't any joy. There's more to life than just getting through. At least…Rafe, I hope so much that there would be. Because I have spent a very long time just getting through. I was never able to just become hard. I insulated myself. Like somebody wrapping a heavy coat around themselves and walking through a storm. But I want more than that for myself now."

"And you think I'm offering you nothing more than survival? I would think that my castle was better than a storm."

She sighed heavily, then smoothed a bandage over his skin. "I didn't lack luxurious surroundings when I was growing up. We've already discussed this."

"Yes. You compared this experience to growing up with your father. And yet I find that it is not so. I have never threatened your safety."

He was surprised when a cool hand touched the side of his face. "But it's not freedom, is it?"

"And what would you do with freedom, *cara mia*?"

"I'm not going to take your children away from you. At a certain point, you will have to trust that."

"Trust is not a simple thing for me."

"Why not?"

She moved back to his knee, removing her hand from his face.

"We grew up in poverty, Mother and I. After we were thrown out of my father's house."

He felt her stiffen. "What?"

"My father threw us out of his house. When his wife returned."

It was silent, her hands moving over his knee, brisk, cool and certain. He wanted to know who else she had bandaged. Another man? He would kill him. Children? Imagining her with children made it feel like his chest was breaking open.

"I didn't know about any of this," she said softly.

"No," he said, keeping his tone casual. "Because I didn't tell you."

"Well. You should have. What did we talk about five years ago, Rafe? How is it we know so little?"

"We were blinded by lust." He laughed. "And now I am just blind."

"I still feel a fair amount of lust," she said, humor lacing her tone.

He reached up, searching for her face. He took hold of her, sliding his thumb over her cheekbone. "Good."

"But you were telling me about your father."

He let his hand fall back down to his side. "The topic of lust is more interesting."

"And lust is the reason we don't know each other."

"My father was a rich man. A married man. He had a house in Rome. And until I was four we lived there. He was not often in, and I had the run of the house. Master of the manor, as it were. But then, he came and told us his family would be moving in. And that meant we had to go."

"He just sent you away with no...provision made for you or anything?"

Rafe shifted beneath her touch, uncomfortable with the topic. He did not like to think about this. Did not like to reflect on it at all. "He was...not deeply involved in my life, you understand. Even when I lived in his home. I was raised primarily by nannies, and I was all the better off for it. But...I loved the house. It was beautiful. And it had so many lovely things in it. I loved to look at them. I was particularly transfixed by a large fish made from carnival glass. It was a whole rainbow of color and movement." He smiled slightly, remembering the trinket. Blue with flashes of purple and green. "I didn't ask to take any toys with me when we left. I asked for that damned fish."

"Oh, Rafe…"

"My father picked it up from the side table where it sat and held it out to me, and as I reached for it, he let it fall. It smashed into a million pieces on the marble floor. Blue, purple, green and destroyed beyond repair."

As he had been in that moment. A small boy, broken, utterly and completely by the rich man who'd fathered him.

"Rafe…how could he…how…?"

"Are you honestly questioning how a father could harm his own child like that? Your father tried to sell you into marriage."

"I know. It says something about me, I guess, that this still shocks me."

"That you are much better than most of the world," he said, his voice rough. "And that our children are lucky to have you."

He did his best not to visualize his father's home. He still remembered it in such detail, and memories were often more invasive now that he didn't have the sight of the world around him to distract him from images of the past.

Still, he could see the marble floors, the rugs he had sat cross-legged on when he was a boy. The large bed he'd sprawled in, like a king. And then after that...

Sleeping on the streets. The beautiful fish smashed to pieces. All his toys gone. His stomach always aching from hunger.

He shoved those thoughts away.

His own children would want for nothing. Of that he could make sure. He had the power now. All of it. And he would not use his power to harm the ones in his care.

But wasn't Charlotte in his care? And wasn't he holding her against her will now?

"You will not leave me," he said, the words much more a rough command than the question he'd intended.

"Rafe, I don't know what I want from life. All of this...the twins... Twins, Rafe. I just...I can't think past them. And here in the castle, at least it's quiet. And I've had a lot of time to myself. It feels like time is standing still here, and in some ways that's good. But one thing I can promise you is this: I will never take your children from you."

"And you?" he asked.

She shouldn't matter. It should be all about the children, and yet, here in his bed he found keeping her was just as important somehow.

"I...I'll stay. For the babies." She added the last part quickly.

But all that mattered was that she had promised to stay.

"My friend, Prince Felipe, is having a party next week."

"What?"

"Was I unclear?" he asked.

"Well, no. But it was an abrupt subject change."

"Not at all," he said, sitting up. "You said you would stay with me. And if you promise to stay with me, then I do not have to keep you here. That means we can go away to Felipe's country and attend his wife's art gallery."

"Oh, well that's very generous of you," she said. He did not miss the sarcasm in her tone.

"I'm not pretending I'm generous. I'm informing you of the change of plans."

"This is your friend who also owns a castle? The reason you had to buy yours?"

"Yes," he said. "Also my other palace-owning friend, Adam, will be there."

"I'm very excited to meet your friends," she said. "I'm excited you have friends."

He growled, grabbing hold of her and pinning her down to the mattress. "I am charming."

"Obviously I'm not immune to you, or I wouldn't be here."

He kissed her, and he could taste the laughter on her lips. "That is good. It is very good." Finally, he was succeeding at his goal. Finally, he had secured her promise she would stay.

He ignored the disquiet in him. Ignored the echoes of other promises he'd heard as a child. That he would be warm tonight. That he would be safe.

That he would always have a home.

He ignored those broken promises and clung to Charlotte.

The problem was that the past looked bright and clear, and the present was full of darkness. But at least she was here. And he could hold her in his arms.

CHAPTER ELEVEN

"RAFE," CHARLOTTE SAID one evening over dinner. "Do you often bring women to events?"

He lifted his head, arching a brow. "Never," he responded.

Charlotte frowned. "Well, do you think that bringing me is going to cause a little bit of a stir?"

"Oh," he said, sounding unconcerned. "Undoubtedly."

"Is my pregnancy a secret?" she pressed.

He raised his shoulders. "Why would it be?"

She held back an exasperated sound. Talking to him was like pulling teeth sometimes. He had all the plans for everything in that brilliant head of his and he seemed to not think sometimes about sharing them with the people they affected.

"I have no idea," she said drily.

"It is not a secret."

She cleared her throat. "How will I be introduced?"

He sighed heavily and reached out, picking up his glass of wine. "As Charlotte Adair, I would suppose."

Charlotte took another bite of her chicken. "All right. Rafe, how come you've never brought women to events before?"

"Because. I haven't been with a woman other than you since my accident."

He said the words so casually, so offhandedly. As he had done every other tiny bit of information given in his short sentences over the course of the meal. But this one...this one held a wealth of information and also raised a thousand questions.

It had never occurred to her that Rafe hadn't been with another woman. He said that she was the last woman he had seen naked, and once he had given context for his accident, that made sense. But that had not meant that she was the last woman he had actually *been* naked with.

"You haven't been with anyone?"

"Neither have you."

"Well. No." But she had been desperately in love with Rafe. And he had broken her heart. Considering she had spent so many years under the impression that he had abandoned her, it had certainly not occurred to her at all that he hadn't moved on. Plus, in the tabloids women did talk about him. Oh, none of them went so far as to claim they had had an affair with him, but they certainly spoke of him in the kinds of reverent tones that one would expect if a man had made them see God. And, she knew from firsthand experience that Rafe possessed that kind of power.

"I just would have thought—"

"I like control," he bit out. "I would have to know someone quite well in my present circumstances in order to have a physical affair with them."

"You didn't know me. When I came up to you at the ball all those weeks ago, it wasn't as if you actually *knew* me."

"Well, failing knowing the person well I

thought perhaps getting you out of my system, finally having some recompense for what happened between the two of us, would fix something inside of me."

"And are you fixed?" she asked.

"Not at all," he responded, his tone dark.

She looked back down at her dinner. "Are you going to be expected to dance with me?" She wanted out of this vein of the conversation. It was oddly painful, and a bit too personal. Because he wasn't telling her what she wanted to hear. What she wanted to hear was that he had abstained from other women because he could not stop thinking about her. Because nobody compared to her.

It was much more likely that he didn't want to be vulnerable with someone after all the physical vulnerability he had endured surrounding his accident.

Still. She liked the fantasy version. One where she mattered.

"We might be," he said. "But I have never done what was expected of me."

"Would you like to?"

"What?"

"You like control, as seems to be the theme of many of our discussions, and our interactions. If you go, and you don't dance, I suppose people understand why. But if you did…"

"You are suggesting that I go all out and surprise people?" he asked.

"You are finally bringing a woman to an event. A woman who happens to be pregnant with your twins. I would think that you might as well go for a triple threat in terms of shocking the world."

Admittedly, she wanted to dance with him.

She wanted to be out in public with him. To not be hiding in her tower room. To not be hiding at all. It had been so long. So many years. Her entire life's worth.

If her future was going to be tied to Rafe's, and it was clear at this point that it was, then she wanted… She wanted it to be bright, beautiful and in the spotlight. She wanted her lover to hold her close on the dance floor, to lay claim to her in public. Without fear of retribution. Yes, her dearest wish was to finally have *everything*.

And for everyone in the whole world to see it.

She had been kept locked away, and then she had been in a prison of her own making. She was tired of that. Tired of living her life dictated by others. By fear.

"Unless you think it would be too difficult," she said, knowing that she was goading him. "Everything can be accomplished through practice. It takes me a bit more practice sometimes than it does others, but I am not afraid of hard work."

"Then I suppose we had better start practicing."

They finished their dinner, and Charlotte suggested they go to the solarium.

"I'm going to move the furniture up against the walls," she said. "I will make sure to let Della know to have it moved back by tomorrow."

"That is fine," he remarked.

"I don't have any music," she said, reaching out and taking hold of his hand.

The corners of his mouth tipped upward, and

she wanted to kiss him. "But you know how to dance?"

"All right, in truth, I've never danced with anyone. But I thought maybe you might know how. You know, since you did go to that fancy private school."

"Your father sent me to private school," he said, his voice deepening, getting rougher, his forehead wrinkling as his brows drew together. "He did not send you to school?"

"I had tutors. I did not go uneducated. He felt that any of the men he might want to marry me off to would not accept a woman with no education at all. But of course, he did not want me too highly educated. Because men don't like that either."

"Your father did damage and in a million inestimable ways, didn't he?"

"I think that we can both agree the most damage was done to you."

"I am not so sure. He used me. Blackmailed me. But he gave me much more freedom than he ever gave you. I think, in some ways, he considered me a son. Though, when a man would hold the threat of death over his own biological child, it is clear that it is not a high compliment to be considered such."

"I suppose he did," she said softly. "No wonder the two of us feel so broken."

"I feel less broken just at the moment," he murmured.

She took a deep breath, trying to shift the weight in her chest. Instead, she felt something like a jagged piece of her soul cut through to her heart. "You do know how to dance?"

"I do." He smiled, the expression somewhat rueful. "Though I have not done so in about thirteen years. And when I did it was under sufferance."

"Well, perhaps it's like riding a bike."

He laughed. "I haven't done that in a long time either."

"We can try," she said. "At least we can try."

He began to lead, his movements firm and strong, and if they weren't moving to any kind of beat, if their steps made no sense, it didn't matter to her. There was no music. There was almost no sound at all.

For him, she knew there was no sight either. And so, she closed her eyes too. Closed her eyes, and trusted him. Allowed him to lead them. Just sweep them both off in this dark, silent dance where she felt as though her feet weren't even touching the ground anymore. She clung to him, her entire body feeling like it was on fire. Her heart feeling like it would burst through the front of her chest.

And when they stopped spinning, when they stopped moving altogether. When it was just the two of them standing there breathing hard, their hearts thundering heavily. She had to acknowledge that shattering sensation in her chest whenever she breathed. To name it for what it was.

Love.

She loved Rafe Costa. And in all likelihood had never stopped loving him. No matter that he had broken her heart. No matter that he had left her—or so she'd believed. No matter that there were five years standing between them, five years of lost time, and so much pain was an uphill climb.

She loved him, and she always had. The evidence was in the simple fact that she had not been able to cut her hair. And also in the fact that she had not been able to take it down for him since they had found each other again.

Because it felt like a symbol of all they had been. The way she had revealed it to him, only to him. How it had felt like a gift, rather than something she was forced to keep because her father considered it an asset.

"I think that will do," she said softly.

"Perhaps it will be much harder when there are other people on the dance floor," he pointed out.

She hadn't thought of that. Of course, in an empty room, they had both been able to close their eyes.

"You lead," she said, "and I will follow. Everyone else can get out of the way."

He smiled, and Charlotte felt as though she had won something. Won back something she had thought lost forever.

In those dark, lonely years she'd spent in hiding she had not imagined she would ever find Rafe again. She had not imagined being with him. She had certainly not imagined that she would be having his children. But they had found each other. They had, and this was the outcome. It was a miracle in many ways, so perhaps they would get one more miracle. Perhaps they could be happy together. He might learn to trust. He might learn to love.

It was an unlikely thing, and she knew it. But, she supposed, it was no more unlikely than their beautiful dance in the dark. And that had happened. So perhaps, the rest would happen too.

"Rafe," she said softly, "I'm ready for bed."

CHAPTER TWELVE

RAFE HAD NEVER been one for large parties. He had always felt somewhat out of place. At the boarding school he had attended with his friends, he was one of the only students who was not from an aristocratic background. Yes, there were some from new money, but most had come from the aristocracy. Princes, like Adam and Felipe. Plus a host of lesser nobles, lords and other obscure titles.

But as far as he knew he was the only one who had come up straight from the gutter. And he had always been aware of the fact that it wasn't through any merit that he was there.

No, he had done nothing good to find himself in this place. Nothing at all. In fact, he had committed a crime, and been taken in as the indentured servant of a crime lord. So, his background had never been anything he had shared freely.

Rafe had always been aware of the inequality, and he was still aware of it. Even now that the money he had was his own, he was aware of it.

There would always be something that distinguished him from everyone else. It had been his humble beginnings at school, and now, it was his blindness. Whatever the reason, these sorts of things had never been his cup of tea, and now he had to go to them even more often than before, because of his status. And because Felipe never took no for an answer.

At least he had Charlotte by his side.

If nothing else, because he had the night after the party to look forward to.

He held on to her hand as they ascended the steps of the museum and walked in. Charlotte leaned over, murmuring softly, "This is a great, open room. It is quite full of people. You can probably hear that."

"Yes," he said, tightening his hold on both her and his cane. "I can."

He could also do a fairly good job of gauging the size of the room based on the acoustics. It was not perfect, but it was educated, at least.

"There are a few tables set up in here, and waiters holding trays of drinks and food. There are a couple of sculptures. Mostly of people. I assume this is the classical art of the country. Your friend was talking about that being part of the exhibition, wasn't he?"

"Yes," Rafe said. "His new wife, Briar, is quite fascinated by art. And when they married, she was put in charge of resurrecting the arts in this country. She brought a great many pieces long thought destroyed out of basements in manor houses and old universities. And she has now done her first exhibition of original art, as well."

"Wow," Charlotte said, feeling a twinge of something.

Could it be jealousy? Envy? That made her feel small and slightly petty, but it was the most likely feeling. It was just that a young woman having such an effect on her adopted country—having such drive—was enviable as far as Charlotte was concerned. Her life had been reduced to survival for so long, and she had so rarely had the chance to make her own decisions.

"She must be quite an amazing woman," Charlotte said.

"She is. She also happens to be the long-lost princess of a country."

"Really?" Charlotte asked.

She supposed she was a long-lost daughter of a crime lord, but that was not anywhere near as glamorous.

She looked across the room and saw a striking couple, a tall, elegantly dressed man in a black suit with his black hair slicked back. By his side, a petite brown-skinned woman with full, curly hair and a shimmering golden ball gown that set off her complexion.

"There is a very good-looking man. Tall. Black haired and an easy smile standing at one o'clock. And next to him is an extremely beautiful woman wrapped in gold."

"I would imagine that is Felipe and Briar. Felipe draws the eye of women quite effortlessly."

"Well," Charlotte said, "my eye is drawn."

"I have, of course, never actually seen his wife, but he is never anywhere without her, so I suspect that is the woman standing next to him."

"They have just been joined by another couple," she said. "But this man is not as handsome. He is…well, he has terrible scars. The woman is pregnant."

"That is Prince Adam Katsaros. And I would assume he is with his wife, Belle. Adam had a terrible accident some years ago. You might say it runs in our group of friends. Only Felipe has escaped unscathed. But then, I suspect Felipe is only unscathed in a physical sense. Though, I think his wife has gone a long way in healing those wounds."

That Rafe could acknowledge that made Charlotte feel hopeful. That he could see that his friends had been healed by the power of the love they had found with their wives. Perhaps, then he would acknowledge that it could be the same for him. Maybe. Just maybe.

"Do you suppose we should go and talk to them?"

He laughed. "I have no doubt. And, if we didn't, Felipe would certainly cause a scene."

"Well," she said, "we don't want to cause a scene. Until we are ready to."

He laughed, and that made her feel like she was doing the right things. Like she had accomplished something. It made her feel as though she might be closer to her goal than she had thought before.

She took his arm, and the two of them walked to where his friends were standing.

His scarred friend Adam kept his emotions carefully guarded, while Felipe looked at them with open interest. The women were smiling, and introductions were made all around.

Charlotte felt…well, it made her yearn. For things she didn't have. For a chance to be a normal couple. A real couple like the two in front of them.

"So is this the missing piece to the puzzle?" Felipe asked.

"Puzzle?" Charlotte asked.

"The puzzle that is Rafe," Felipe said. "He has always been incredibly quiet about certain aspects of his past. The time that we had no contact with him between school and adulthood. I have always assumed that there was a woman involved. And I see now that I was correct."

"You don't know that she's from my past," Rafe said. "I didn't say."

"I suppose I don't know. But my intuition is pretty good. And, you have never brought a woman with you to any event like this. As far as I know, you have essentially lived like a monk for the past five years. You are welcome to correct me if I'm wrong."

Rafe looked annoyed for a moment, then schooled his expression into one that was carefully controlled. "Very well. Charlotte is a woman I've known for a great many years."

"Did you kidnap her? Because you were exceedingly judgmental when Adam and I kidnapped our wives."

"Did they kidnap you?" Charlotte addressed Belle and Briar, who exchanged long-suffering looks, then nodded.

"Well, Adam took me prisoner, technically," Belle said.

"Felipe definitely kidnapped me. From a hospital."

Charlotte blinked. "Well." She cleared her throat. "I'm not his wife."

"But are you kidnapped?" Felipe asked. "In my opinion that is the most important bit of information."

"Not anymore," Charlotte answered.

"Not anymore," Adam said drily. "So you did kidnap her."

"Unbelievable," said Felipe, shaking his head. "You would think that two princes and a billionaire would be able to find wives without having to resort to force."

"I'm not his wife," Charlotte repeated.

"So you said," Felipe responded.

"Though, you should be the first to hear," Rafe said, "that Charlotte and I are having twins."

Adam's eyebrows shot up, and Felipe grinned. "Congratulations."

"Congratulations is the right sentiment, yes?" Adam asked.

"Yes," he responded, sounding annoyed now.

It was a funny thing to see Rafe with friends. She had never imagined him having any. Because at her father's he was in a very isolated place, as was she. And in the time since she had continued to be isolated, so even though tabloid stories had painted a different picture, she had imagined him that way in some regards. Yes, she had imagined him with lovers, but not with relationships.

"Well, we do expect to be invited to the wedding," Felipe said. "Since, as you continue to point out, she is not your wife. Which means she will be eventually."

"He hasn't asked me," Charlotte said.

That earned him heated glares from the women.

"It was nice to meet you, Charlotte." Princess Briar extended her hand. "I have to go and make the rounds now. As is expected of me. But we will see each other again, I think."

The princess gave a slight curtsy, then wandered back into the throng.

Felipe chuckled. "I had better make the rounds too. I must ensure that my wife is adequately fêted. As is fitting of her status." He walked off then, following Princess Briar's path.

Leaving Charlotte and Rafe with the darker, quieter presence of his friends Adam and Belle.

"I think I need something to eat," Belle said, looking apologetic. "And drink. It's hot in here."

Charlotte felt like she was looking into her future just then.

"Of course," Adam said, his expression one of concern. He was so clearly besotted with his bride, it warmed Charlotte. And only made her slightly jealous.

He left then, and that left Charlotte alone with Rafe.

"Your friends seem nice," she said. "Surprisingly so. All things considered."

"Which things considered?"

"Your personality?"

He laughed. "You don't seem to mind it."

"I don't." She looped her arm through his, and they walked through the gallery and into the first room that was set up for dancing. The music was playing, swelling around them, and her heart began to beat faster. "Dance with me?"

"We have practiced for it, have we not?" He paused next to the wall, and leaned his cane up against it before tightening his hold on her.

"Yes, we have."

And then he was the one leading her out onto the dance floor, blazing a path through the crowd, a man who clearly expected for everyone else to part the way for him, so that he would have no concerns about where he should stand. "I suppose we are about to make that scene we were just discussing."

"Possibly." She put her hand on his face. "That's why they'll stare."

"Or they will probably stare if I step on people."

"Well, likely not. You're a powerful billionaire, after all. They would probably just decide that they should step on people too. You know, in case it's a trend."

Then they were moving, and in perfect time with the music. Charlotte kept her eyes open this time, making sure that they didn't actually step on anyone. People were watching them. Probably because Rafe Costa never brought women out in public. And possibly because he was dancing. But she didn't care why. She only cared that she was finally out with the man that she loved. Being held in his arms for all the world to see. That there was nothing to hide, nothing to be ashamed of. That this was a moment denied her for so many years, finally happening now.

Maybe she didn't have a grand plan. Maybe she didn't have drive like Prince Felipe's wife. But she had this. And it was new, and special, different. She had that great, ill-fated love. The one that had broken her heart. The one that had broken the man she had cared for. They had kept it hidden, and had touched only ever in secret.

But not now. Not this time. It made it all feel bright. New and possible.

He spun her, then brought her back into his body, his hold firm, his steps unerring. He spun her until she was dizzy, breathless, until they might as well be the only people in the room, as they had been back in his castle.

Then, with every eye on them, they walked through the ballroom hand in hand, into the art gallery.

He stood behind her, his hands placed possessively on her stomach. He bent down, whispered in her ear. "Tell me about the paintings."

"This one here, directly in front of us, is an evening scene. There are rolling hills set behind a large, expansive field. Nestled into the hills are houses. There are lights on in the windows. It's probably dinnertime. Dark outside but not late enough to sleep. Families all gathered around the table. I bet it's winter. And early. Cold the way that those evenings get, where the chill bites into your skin. And the warmth in the house makes your cheeks tingle when you go inside. All of these people that live in the houses, I bet they have families they're sitting with. Talking to. Telling them about their days."

"You see all that?" he asked, his voice gruff.

"I don't know. Not really, I guess. It made me feel it, though."

"Even if I had my sight I don't think I would see that," he said. "I would just see lights on in houses. Not families. Not happy homes. That you still have the ability to imagine such things, that you do it so easily, is nothing short of a miracle."

"I don't feel very special," she said. "Or very miraculous. I'm only Charlotte. I haven't…put together an amazing gallery like the princess here. I haven't done anything at all. I was set free, and the first thing I did was come to find you."

She looked up at him, and saw that his face had gone pale.

"Rafe," she said, "what is it?"

"Nothing," he responded. "Though I do believe you're the first person other than your father—who wanted me dead—to ever seek me out. And so, I would not call it nothing."

They continued walking down the hall, and she continued to describe the scenes in the paintings for him. She did so until her throat ached, until her feet were tired. And until she was about ready to fall asleep standing up.

"We had a long day of travel," Rafe said, "and I know that Felipe has set aside a room for us. Perhaps, it is time we went back to the palace?"

"My second palace in only a couple of weeks. It all feels quite extravagant."

"I should like you to have extravagance. Though, every time I promise you extravagance you remind me that your father gave it to you, as well, and that it was little more than a comfortable prison. And so, I'm at a loss as to how to present you with such things."

"Being with you is not a prison," she said, feeling guilty, because he was right. He had offered her things, and she continually played them down. Because they weren't what she wanted, not really. She wanted him. He was very willing to give things, but he held parts of himself back.

So controlled was his existence. So controlled

was he. She wanted more, but she had a feeling that were she to ask for more he would claim he had already given everything.

She allowed him to guide her back to the front of the museum, and she waited as he spoke to a man out front about getting them a car. They rode in silence back to the palace.

Once they arrived, they were escorted to a side entrance that led them the most direct route to a room—or rather a series of rooms—that was tucked back behind all of the others. It felt like a private little retreat. Something intimate enclosed inside the mammoth space.

Once the doors closed behind them, Rafe turned his focus to her, his dark eyes glittering. And she saw it there. The spark of something completely uncontrolled. Wild. Animal even. She felt goose bumps rise up on her skin, and her entire body shivered beneath his unseeing gaze.

"I have but one request, darling Charlotte," he said, his voice hard. "Let down your hair."

And this time, Charlotte wanted nothing more than to comply. She wanted to give him this. Give it to him with all of herself, with no coercion at all. Because all this time she had saved that hair for Rafe. And she had held it back over the past weeks because she had been holding back her heart. But if she wanted all of him, then she could hold nothing of herself in reserve.

She could no longer protect herself.

She was—in so many ways—jaded. Her own father had not loved her. Had treated her like a thing. A prize pawn in a game. She had been emotionally abused. Had lost the only man she had ever loved—imagined herself abandoned by him. And then she had spent five years living in a strange kind of isolation.

But she also felt...so green, so inexperienced. As if life held a great many wonders that she had not yet seen. That she was desperate to see.

She didn't know how she could hold both of those feelings inside of her. Both the bone-deep sense of world weariness and a fascination with the same world.

But she did. It was all a part of her, whether it made sense or not.

She reached up and worked one of her hairpins free, allowing the pin to drop to the floor as one silken curl unwound itself and fell, thick and heavy down her back.

A muscle in his jaw ticked, his expression going hard as stone.

Then she removed another pin, and another, letting them all drop to the floor, the small sound swelling in the otherwise silent room.

Her hair fell in long, heavy coils, the blond waves falling down well past her waist. Hair that had felt like a burden, that had felt like part of her imprisonment, something that belonged to her father and never to her, until Rafe.

Until he had changed it. Changed her. Changed her entire perception on the world.

"Only for you, my prince," she said, once the task was finished.

She didn't wait for him to come to her. Instead, she moved across the space and wrapped her arms around his neck, pressed a kiss to his lips. He lifted his hands, threading them through her hair, winding around his fist, holding tight and tugging as he tilted her head back and deepened his exploration of her mouth, his tongue sliding against hers, his teeth scraping the edge of her lower lip.

She moaned, reveling in this, in this prelude to something that she knew was going to destroy her. Change her irrevocably. And even knowing that, she couldn't regret it. Didn't want to stop it.

She wanted all of this, all of him. Every single thing that he would offer, she would take.

And perhaps, that was her gift. Perhaps that was her. The thing that made her special. This ability to love, this ability to hope in spite of all that she had been through. It had seemed like nothing. Like something commonplace. And yet, having met his friends, having seen Rafe himself, she knew that it was not. Love and hope could be burned out of a person by the dark, cruel things in the world.

And that she had been subjected to some of the worst of it, and yet had continued to hold it in her heart. While she was in exile. Even knowing that it was doomed, she had fallen in love with Rafe.

Had continued to love him deep inside of herself in spite of what she had thought to be a betrayal.

She knew that she could be a mother to her children. Knew that she would love them unconditionally, with unfettered grace in spite of the transgressions that had been committed against her by her own father.

In spite of the fact that she had never known a mother, she knew that she could be one.

She had not considered those gifts. She had not considered it having a sense of direction for her life. And yet it was. It was a miraculous thing, a wonderful thing, and it'd been inside of her all along. Opening herself up now, allowing him all of her, allowing him this moment, this moment of reckless love that she wanted to pour out on him regardless of what he might give in return, made her feel more whole, more complete than she could remember ever feeling.

It was a risk. And she knew it. But it was necessary. Without this. This freely given gift. This wild and reckless love, she would always be in a cage. A cage of her own making. She refused to give her father that. Refused to give that to her stepmother. She refused to let them beat her.

She refused to be hidden.

She had stood in the light earlier with Rafe on the dance floor, so she would stand in it now. With him.

"I want you to tell me about this beautiful dress while I take it off your exquisite body," he murmured against her lips.

"Of course," she complied. "It's a dark, rich purple, with long sleeves that fall off the shoulder. There is a zipper in the back."

He reached around behind her, taking hold of the zipper and lowering it slowly.

"The skirt flows away from my body. Doesn't give very much away. It's quite discreet."

"I like that. That I am the keeper of your secrets."

She looked up at him, pressed her thumb to the line on one side of his mouth and smoothed it. "You are. And I hope that I am yours."

He said nothing to that. Instead, he released his

hold on her hair and pushed the rich velvet dress from her body and consigned it to the floor.

"What about your underwear?" he asked.

"That...is less discreet. I chose them thinking about describing them to you. They're black. And thin."

As if to test her claims he lifted his hand, brushing his thumb over her nipple, achingly sensitive through the sheer lace bra.

Then he unhooked it, and moved his hands down over her curves, to her hips, pulling her panties down and discarding them too.

Then he turned her around abruptly so that she was facing away from him and pressing his hand between her shoulder blades, stroking all the way down, over her back, over the silken curtain of her hair.

"So beautiful," he said. "So soft. It is like silk in my hands. And if I remember right, it is the color of raw spun gold. I dreamed of this. Of touching you like this. You and all your soft, incredible beauty. Your hair, which is like no other woman's ever."

"I kept it for you," she said, feeling like now was the time to tell him that. Now that she was no longer holding back. "Only for you."

"Because you knew I liked it?"

"Yes," she said. "Because something inside of me refused to give us up. In spite of what I had been told. In spite of…everything. There was a large part of my heart that could never let go of you."

And it never will.

But she didn't speak that last part out loud.

He gathered her hair up into his hand, twisted it around his fist again. Then he drew her up against his body, and she could feel the hard, insistent arousal pressed against her rear.

She gasped, wiggling against him, feeling as though she would die if she didn't have him. All of him. His hands, his skin. His full possession.

She was naked, and he was still fully clothed. It felt far too real. A too-honest appraisal of the entire situation. That she was ready to expose herself. Utterly and completely, and he was still holding back.

But she had no time to protest. He leaned in, his voice rough, fractured. "Tell me about the layout of the room."

She could hardly think, let alone offer him a description of the space. But, she did her best to gather her thoughts. To do as he asked. "The bed is directly in front of us," she said. "Over to your right is a door, I assume that leads into the bathroom."

"Is there a vanity?"

"Yes," she responded. "To the left, in the center of the far wall. There is."

Keeping his hold on her, he began to move in the direction she'd said the vanity was in. "Take us to it," he asked her roughly. She complied. Moving to stand in front of it.

"Brace your hands on the top," he commanded.

She complied, pressing her palms flat against the shining mahogany surface, her heart thundering as she did. She heard him working his belt, then undoing the zipper on his pants.

He coiled her hair more tightly around his fist, pulled tight, so that her head was forced backward. She looked at their reflection. Rafe, looming large and dark behind her, looking like an avenging angel. The sight of her pale, bare body in the mirror, with his hands gripping her hips tight enough to leave marks behind on her skin made her entire body shiver with erotic anticipation.

This was something that probably would have frightened her five years ago. Something that would have reminded her of being tethered. Being held back. But, with all of her recent revelations, it didn't bother her at all. It excited her. Because she knew her own power here. With him. She knew exactly what she wanted. And she knew that even though he was the one with all the physical strength, that he was the one holding her tight, pinning her in this submissive position, that she possessed her own kind of strength.

That she had the power to bring this man to his knees.

Only she didn't want that.

He had been brought to his knees already. Had been wounded. Betrayed. Left for dead by both

of the men who had played the part of father figure in his life.

She would not ask that of him.

She would never require it.

He positioned himself at the entrance of her
body, rocking his hips forward, pressing her more
firmly against the edge of the vanity.

"I want you to watch us," he said. "There is a
mirror, yes?"

"Yes," she said, her voice trembling.

"Watch us," he commanded. "Tell me what you
see."

He thrust completely inside of her, and she
gasped, looking up as he had asked her to do.
"I…"

He thrust harder, increasing the pace, and
though she wanted to obey him, she didn't know
where to begin. Didn't know what to say. The
woman looking back at her was clearly in the
throes of ecstasy. Her cheeks a heightened color,
her eyes glistening with need.

Her breasts moved each time he thrust into her
body, her nipples tight. And then there was him.

Big, muscular and perfect. His dark eyes were full of black fire, his jaw tight, his teeth clenched, his lips curled into a near snarl.

She lowered her head, resting her cheek on the cool surface, trying to cool her heated skin. She waited for him to reprimand her, but it didn't come.

She moaned as he claimed her, over and over. The wood bit into her skin, and her scalp prickled. He pulled her hair hard, forcing her to look back up at her reflection in the mirror. She probably would have looked like an angel falling from grace to anyone who saw her now.

But she thought it looked a lot more like finding salvation. Finding freedom. There was nothing here to be ashamed of. Nothing here to hide.

When she made helpless sounds of pleasure, she wasn't ashamed. When the furniture hit the wall as he thrust home, she only wanted more. Wanted the whole room to fall apart around them. A testament to the changing landscape inside of her.

To them changing their surroundings, rather than being changed by them.

They had been locked up for too long.

"Take me," she whispered. "Please. Harder. I need you."

He growled, complying, his movements becoming uncontrolled. Almost violent. And she reveled in it. In the shades that came with making love. The uncivilized. The base and raw. The soft and beautiful. Gentle and rough. Pleasurable and painful.

He stopped, suddenly, withdrawing from her body and turning her, then picking her up. "Direct me to the bed," he growled.

"Straight behind you," she said, breathless, her legs like jelly.

Without Rafe holding her she would have melted completely to the floor.

He crossed the room slowly, and she told him when he'd reached the edge of the bed. He laid them both down, brought her down on top of him, her hair shielding them both, falling down over his chest.

He reached up, stroking her hair, threading it through his fingers. "My whole world is darkness," he rasped. "But when you're with me. When I'm in you, I see light again. And it doesn't matter that it's not out here. It doesn't matter that it's only in my mind. It's the only light I have."

A tear slid down her cheek, and she was grateful that he couldn't see it. Because he wouldn't like her crying for him. Not even a little. Not at all. He would get angry and tell her that he wasn't fragile. And he wasn't. She knew.

Charlotte rocked up and down on his body, driving them both wild. Taking them closer to the edge of madness. Tears flowed freely from her eyes as pleasure twisted inside her stomach, unleashing a tidal wave inside of her.

His hold on her hips was nearly painful, but she didn't mind. She welcomed it. Welcomed the lack of control. Welcomed the way that he growled as he thrust deep inside. Welcomed the swear words in both English and Italian that fell from his lips as easily and readily as endearments and encouragements.

Her world was shrunk down once again. And the only people in it were Rafe and herself. That should frighten her. Because she had lived in a shrunken world before. But it wasn't full like this one. And it wasn't her choice. This was a world of her own making.

A world of their making.

And it wasn't about control. It wasn't about stifling, limiting or oppressing. It was about love. At least for her, it was about love.

Her release shuttered over her like a pane of glass, the glitter dust shimmering all around her, through her, cutting deep into her skin, and her soul, with the brilliant kind of terrible beauty that went on and on as she pulsed around his hardness.

His own release came on a feral growl as he slammed her body down on his while thrusting up, spending himself deep within her.

She collapsed over him, going limp against his chest, her hair a tangled cloud of silk around them. He stroked it, sliding his fingers through the golden strands. She closed her eyes, reveling in the feeling. The way that he touched her made her feel precious. It didn't make her feel owned. Didn't make her feel as if she were a thing.

In his arms, with an uncertain future and a pain in her chest, she felt more herself than she ever had.

Back when she had been eighteen, when she and Rafe had been little more than children, at least emotionally, she had been lost and saw what it meant to be in love from her point of view alone. The excitement, the danger. It had been real, but it had been one-dimensional.

He had also been the only man in the vicinity. That was not the case now. She had spent five years traveling all around, and in that time she'd found no one that appealed to her in the same way that Rafe did. She had gone to London to seek him out. She had made her choice. He might have kidnapped her and taken her to a castle; pregnancy might have, from certain points of view, forced them together.

Except, there was no force involved. Not really. She had chosen Rafe a long time ago. And the way things had played out over the past few months had only confirmed that.

Another tear fell from her eyes, landing on his chest, and this time she knew he would be aware of it. But that was okay. It might make him angry, but then she would simply deal with his anger. Because she wasn't here for happiness alone. She wasn't here simply to please him. That wasn't love.

Love was all of it. All of him, and all of her. Yes, certain parts of him were jagged and rough, and bits of her were cynical, while some remained woefully inexperienced. But together, she was confident that they could find a way to fit.

That they could find a way to be everything. For each other. And for themselves.

"Rafe," she whispered, pressing a kiss to his chest. "I love you."

Rafe felt as if the world was crashing down around him. Breaking off into tiny pieces that he could not collect as quickly as they were undoing themselves. He felt as if the very walls around them were caving in.

He moved away from Charlotte, jackknifing into a sitting position, his heart pounding so hard he thought it might explode.

"You do not love me," he said, the denial ripped from him.

"Oh, really? I don't? Why do you suppose I'm here with you, Rafe? Do you think it's just because I like castles? Or have I not made my position on those things clear?"

"You have. But what you feel isn't love."

"Oh, really?" She sounded angry now, and he supposed he couldn't blame her. But there was a desperate beast roaming through his chest, and he could not control it or stop it. He hated that. Hated that this made him feel not only out of control but utterly and completely at the mercy of something that he could not see or touch with his hands.

Vision would not have helped in this moment. Even with his sight he could not have dealt with this any easier.

Love. Love was pain. It was only ever that. It was only ever false hope.

A beautiful glass figurine held up in front of you and then smashed onto the floor just as it was being placed in your hands.

A body that functioned just fine until it was pushed over the edge of the balcony and smashed on the ground below. As if it was glass, just like that long-ago statue.

He was far too familiar with this brand of pain. Far too familiar with the ultimate end.

How many times did a man have to be shown the fate of love before he began to believe it?

The end of love—and there was always an end—was pain. Always. And forever.

"I do not love you," he said, his voice hard. "So you can call it whatever you wish, and you can demand whatever you want, but you will not get those words from me, Charlotte Adair."

"That doesn't make any sense," she said. Of course, his Charlotte would not let this go easily. She never did. She was inquisitive, and she poked at him. She always had.

She had no sense. Any other woman who had
spent her life under the autocratic rule of a madman would be much more afraid of him; that was
certain. She would be much less likely to speak
her mind, much less likely to risk herself, and yet
Charlotte seemed to have never taken on board
the fact that her spirit should be dented, if not
crushed after her experiences.

The foolish woman.

She had no sense to protect herself.

And it made no sense to him. None at all.

"It doesn't need to make sense to you in order
for it to be," he said. "What is love, Charlotte?
When has it ever served either of us?"

"Will you not love your children, Rafe? And
if not, then what is the point of laying claim to
them? What was the point of laying claim to me?
Just to keep us as possessions? In that case, how
are you different from my father? You profess
that you're not like him. You swear it to me. And
yet, if all you want to do is have me so that you
can control me, have your children so that you
can control them, how does that not become the

same twisted thing that my father had. At the end of all the years, how do you keep it from turning into something sadistic?" She moved away from him, and he felt the bed shift, assumed that she had gotten out of it. He heard bare feet on the stone floor, and it confirmed his suspicions. "I have come to the conclusion that love is the thing that keeps us all human. It is the thing that makes us free. Brave. Good. Otherwise we turn inward. If we cannot love, we become small, selfish things who look out only for our self-interest."

"Self-interest is important," he said. "Without it, God knows I would be dead."

"But it can't be the only thing. Self-interest is the kind of thing that spurs men to build empires that do nothing but wound and oppress. Self-interest is what creates men like my father. Love is what destroys them."

"Then perhaps I am more like your father than we think, because all love has ever done is destroy me."

"Rafe..."

"I loved my father. I loved our life. I loved our

home. And yet, in the end it netted me nothing except pain. I loved you. And what did it get me?" He laughed, a short, humorless sound. "You say that love gives, but in my experience it only takes. I nearly died for our love, and what did it get me? Where were you in the end? You believed in my defection so easily."

"And you believed in mine. But you have such a convenient out here, Rafe, that I can have this argument with you. I was hiding. Afraid for my life. You were physically wounded and absolutely unable to come for me. And I understand that. But the minute…the minute I was no longer afraid for my life I came for you. It was the first thing that I did."

He gritted his teeth, shame lashing at him. To accuse Charlotte of abandoning him was unfair all things considered. But he did not feel fair. He felt…broken and raging, and utterly helpless to do anything to stop it.

"What does love matter, Charlotte? In the end, what does it matter?"

There was a pause, and then she made a small,

choked sound. "It's everything. Don't you understand that? It's absolutely everything."

"I understand that it was the key component in the most terrible losses I have suffered. Me believing myself to be loved. Trusting in that. Trusting anyone but myself. I believe in money. I believe in things I can create. Things I can control. Nothing else."

"Can you believe in me, Rafe?"

And he knew. That in many ways he was standing on the edge of that balcony again. Teetering on the edge. That this was one of those moments that would either build something or destroy it. And he had a choice to make.

But he had been bruised. He had been abandoned. And he had fallen.

He could not submit himself to that again.

"I can't," he said, his voice rough.

He heard the soft rustle of fabric, and he knew that she was getting dressed. Knew that she was getting ready to leave him. And it enraged him.

"So," he said, his voice hard, "you love me, and yet you're going to leave me. Abandon me, because I cannot give you exactly what you've asked for. How is that love, Charlotte? It seems a weak and selfish thing."

He heard shoes on the floor, and he knew that she was ready to leave. That no amount of striking out at her now was going to stop her.

"I don't know," she said. "Maybe it is. All I know is that I have lived in the tower before, Rafe. Alone. Isolated. I have shrunk myself down, hidden my heart. And I just don't want to do it anymore. I do love you. But I don't think staying with you and pretending that I don't is going to do either of us any favors. And I think right now loving you has to mean walking away. Because in order to love you the way that I want to, the way that I need to, I need to take care of myself. My own heart. I need to do that for our children too. I will never block you from seeing them—you have to understand that. I am not taking them from you. But I am taking myself away. Because I can't..."

She took a deep breath, and he imagined what

she must look like standing there. Frail but strong. And it broke him.

"I can't hide anymore," she continued. "I can't go back. Having now opened myself up I can't close myself off again. And I won't. This world is so cruel. It's hard and it isn't fair. But I...I'm brave enough to love you knowing that. I feel very much like I deserve the same. Like I shouldn't have to accept something less."

And then, she was gone. He heard her footsteps carrying her farther and farther away. And he sat there for a moment, unable to decide what to do.

Then he stood, righting his clothes, hastily making it so that everything important was covered before flinging the door open and tearing off down the hall.

He didn't have his cane. He didn't know which direction she had gone. He strained his ears listening for the sound of her footsteps, but he could hear nothing. Nothing.

And the darkness closed in around him. Charlotte had been his light, and now she was gone. He had no idea what in hell he was supposed to do now. How he was going to survive. How he was going to move on.

The simple fact of the matter was he didn't want to. He wanted to have her with him. Wanted to have her love him without having to give anything up in return. Because that's all love could ever be to him. Loss.

But this loss was one far beyond any of the others he had experienced. When he had fallen from the tower, he had been left broken and bleeding, in very much the literal sense. But he felt it just as keenly now. Like he was going to bleed out onto the stone floor of the castle, his heart a ravaged, damaged thing that was hemorrhaging with every beat.

He heard movement, and he began to run. But he did not realize there was a staircase until he was falling.

He struck his temple on the edge of something hard, and a blast of pain shot through his skull, down his spine. And for a moment, he knew nothing. Felt nothing.

And when he came back to himself and opened his eyes, a shaft of light broke the darkness.

CHAPTER THIRTEEN

CHARLOTTE WASN'T HIDING from him. And thankfully, he hadn't come after her. Or, she tried to tell herself that she was thankful about that. Really. It kind of hurt.

Because of course initially he had kidnapped her and dragged her to a castle in Germany. Now she was just sitting at her flat in London, right where Rafe could easily find her if he wanted to, and he hadn't.

Her love really was repellent, apparently.

At least her morning sickness was starting to abate a tiny bit. So, there was that. Of course, she still didn't want to get out of bed.

She had been heartbroken by Rafe before. But this was different. Because this had been her choice.

She could have stayed with him forever. She

could have stayed with him, and she could have tried to make herself be all right with the fact that he didn't love her back. She could have kept her love hidden. Could have kept it quiet, never spoken of it. She could have made it the nonissue that it was.

But she hadn't done that.

She had demanded love. Had demanded it, insisted upon it, and had refused to hide the love she felt for him.

It hurt so badly that convincing herself it was a good thing was difficult, but in her heart, she knew it was right.

She took a deep breath and opened up her laptop. She had been looking into some things. Enrolling in classes.

It would be difficult with the twins; she knew it would be. But she wasn't destitute, and she needed to figure some things out.

She couldn't sit around and do nothing.

Well, she supposed she could, but she would go insane. She needed to have some focus, a goal. She needed to at least figure out what she was interested in. Because she had spent so much of her life unable to do that.

Perhaps she could do some online schooling while the twins were little. It would give her a chance to find out about what she might want, and that would be helpful. And her education had been so tightly controlled by her father, it would be good for her to expand her horizons.

She wanted to stay in London, of course, because no matter that Rafe had broken her heart, she needed to be in proximity for the sake of the children.

She felt a stab in her chest. She was going to be a mother, but she was not going to have a husband. And actually, the husband part didn't really matter. She didn't want some generic groom that could be any old cake topper. She wanted Rafe. As her husband, as her boyfriend, as her captor. Pretty much any way she could get him.

But she had walked away from him.

She had demanded love, in spite of the fact that part of her wasn't even certain yet she deserved it. She had certainly never been given it freely in her life.

Rafe, in fact, had been the only person to give it to her easily. But that had been five years ago, and when her stepmother had killed the dream of the two of them being together, when she had taken his sight from him, she had apparently stolen that last bit of his ability to love, as well.

She hated her for that. Hated her and hated her father. And hated Rafe's father for good measure. For throwing him out. For breaking a beautiful thing Rafe loved out of spite. But all of that hate didn't fix it.

But then, her love didn't either, so she felt that reserving a small corner of her heart for anger at those particular people was fair enough.

She took a deep breath, and looked out the window. She still had seven and a half months before the babies would be born. And she really did need to find something to occupy herself.

She wasn't locked in this apartment. She wasn't locked up anywhere.

Resolutely, she walked toward her front door

and put on a long winter coat. Then she grabbed her plaid scarf and tossed it over her shoulders, wrapping it around her neck.

She made her way down to the city streets, doing her best to enjoy the cheer and sparkle of the Christmas decorations that were already beginning to go up in late November.

She didn't feel very cheerful, but the city looked cheerful. And she had the freedom to move about in it as she chose. So, she supposed there was something cheering in that.

She kept on walking past a row of tall, rusty brick buildings with bold white trim and a beautiful little park. The narrow streets were quiet until they opened up to a larger intersection, and she realized exactly where she'd been wandering all this time.

To her very favorite department store for window-shopping. The large store was bedecked with Christmas lights, and they were like a welcome sign as far as Charlotte was concerned.

Suddenly, she was seized with a bit of inspiration. It was the holidays, and undoubtedly there would be stores that needed more help. She had always enjoyed working in shops. She liked talking to people. It was better than sitting around feeling morose—that was for sure. And all right, maybe it wasn't a long-term plan. Or maybe it was. It was easy to get into this idea that if she didn't perform an entire country's art program, or get higher education that she wasn't doing anything. But she enjoyed working in retail. After so many years by herself it gave her a chance to be with people. It made her happy. When her life had been bleak, it had brought her joy.

Well, her life was damned bleak now.

At least she could look at other people who were smiling for the next few weeks. She could enjoy the hustle and bustle of Christmas. Get out of her own head.

And so, resolute, she marched right beneath the green awnings and into the shop, and decided she was going to ask for a job.

"It's difficult to explain, Mr. Costa, but then your particular injury always was." Rafe's doctor was looking at CAT scan results in front of him. "It seems to me that you injured your brain again in your most recent fall. And that the trauma and swelling of the brain tissue, coupled with this new healing has given your brain the chance to right some of the previous damage."

He stared blankly at the man in front of him. The man with gray hair and deep lines on his face. Dr. Keller was the same physician he'd been going to since he'd first come to London, but he'd never actually *seen* the man before.

He could now. He could see everything.

"So basically," Rafe said, slowly, "it did what you hoped my brain would do on its own in the aftermath of the original accident?"

"Yes."

"Will it reverse itself? As it keeps healing? Will it just go back to how it was?" He'd expected each morning since to open his eyes and be met with darkness. Instead, there had been morning light filtering through his window. And he'd been able to see it.

But Charlotte was still gone.

The doctor lifted a shoulder. "I can't answer that. I don't see why it would, but then, I would not have told you another knock on the head would have fixed your sight, or I would have suggested we hit you with a hammer a long time ago."

The doctor was joking, but Rafe did not feel like laughing.

It had been a week since his fall at the castle had resulted in his first glimpse of light in over five years. A week since Charlotte had left him. And in that time, his vision had been growing steadily clearer. At first, it was just an increase in light and shape. But as the swelling from the impact had receded, his vision had begun to return in force.

His vision still wasn't perfect, or so he was told. It looked good enough to him. But then, his frame of reference wasn't so great, considering he had seen nothing more than vague, muddy gray on black for half a decade.

He should be...he didn't know. He should be happy. He could see light again. But the light in his soul had gone out. Charlotte was gone, and his vision was back. And if there was anything on earth more ironic than that, he could not think of it. As if he had had to lose her in order to gain this.

It hurt. Everything. His head, from the injury. His chest, from the loss of her.

And he knew that he was supposed to sit here and smile and be happy because he was some sort of medical marvel and miracle, just in time for the holiday season. And undoubtedly, once the tabloids seized hold of all of this, he would be expected to give commentary.

He had no commentary. Not for anyone or anything.

He scowled, and did his best to thank the doctor before heading out of the office and back onto the streets. He had chosen to walk today, simply because he could. Without a guide or aid of a cane.

He *hated* the Christmas decorations. The lights strung overhead. It was all a mockery of turmoil that was happening in his soul. The general cheer of the place.

That there was anyone smiling in the world at all when he felt like he did.

It was his own fault that Charlotte had left him, and he knew it. He just…he could not face any more loss. And he had been certain that love was the poison that seemed to generate loss in his life.

But then, Charlotte was gone. She was gone, and it hurt now. Whether or not he had ever said those words to her. Whether or not he had ever truly taken it on board when she had said them. Saying he didn't believe in it. None of it mattered at all. Not when he felt like he was being crushed beneath the weight of his despair.

He walked through the lobby of his building with barely a glance at the opulent settings. A strange thing. But he could hardly be bothered to take in the details of the place that he had not acquired until after he lost his vision.

The one thing he had enjoyed in the ensuing week was the view from his office. He had chosen well. Even if he had chosen out of a kind of petty need to keep something from other rich men. He was enjoying it now. As much as he could enjoy anything.

He got into the gilded lift—which, he thought, was a bit gaudy actually and he was going to have it changed—and pushed the button that would take him up to his office floor.

When he got out, his PA was sitting at the desk looking agitated. "You have visitors," she remarked.

She looked worried, and he was not used to having the sense that his PA was ever worried. But then, he wondered if she was just very good at keeping her voice calm, and if she actually frequently looked worried and he just hadn't known it.

"Why did you allow visitors in? You know I'm not in a good mood."

"Well," she said. "As terrifying as you are, I wasn't really sure how I was going to refuse two princes."

He muttered a vile curse beneath his breath. Of course, Adam and Felipe were here.

"There is, of course, no way you could refuse

either of them. They're royal asses. But I will deal with them. Don't worry."

He passed through the antechamber, and into his office, where Adam—who was indeed hideously scarred—and Felipe were waiting.

"You look terrible," Rafe said by way of greeting.

He had never actually seen his friend since his accident had left him scarred.

"It's true, then," Adam said, his expression fierce. "You can see?"

"Is that the going rumor already? I've only just started to accept it as fact. I didn't realize it was common knowledge."

"It is not common knowledge," Adam said, sounding imperious. "*I* am not common. But Belle was in touch with your housekeeper at the German castle, and, it may have come up."

"I should fire Della for her indiscretion."

"You won't," Felipe said simply, a bit too cheerfully.

"I just might," he returned.

"You can *see*," Adam said, "but you are in a

worse temper than when last I saw you. Which leads me to believe that the other rumor is also true. You have lost your hostage."

"She was not a *hostage*," Rafe said. "But to confirm your suspicions, yes. Charlotte has moved back to her own home."

Charlotte, whom he had made a concerted effort *not* to see since his vision had returned. Were he to actually lay eyes on her, he would lose himself completely. Promise her anything. There were limits to his strength.

"Well, she was with you, and then she was seen running out of my palace very late at night a week ago, and no one has seen her since."

"I'm sure *someone* has seen her since," Rafe said drily.

"This is why Belle was digging around," Adam said. "Because Briar heard that she had fled the castle. They were concerned."

"And none of you thought to ask me?"

"You're a grumpy bastard," Felipe said. "We didn't want to have to talk to you about it until we could force you to."

"Some friends I have."

"The very best," Adam said, his tone hard. "Which is why I'm here to ask you if you're stupid."

"Do I look stupid to you?"

Adam appraised him, his dark eyes hard. "Yes, you do look rather stupid. Because you're standing here without that woman. And she clearly cared for you. Is having your children, and... What did you do?"

"She *left me*," Rafe said, his voice a growl. "I did not send her away. She left of her own free will."

"For no reason?" Felipe asked.

"No reason that truly mattered," Rafe answered.

"Except, clearly it mattered enough for her to leave."

"The two of you, you get married, and you think you know things. But you had to kidnap your wives. So, perhaps you don't know any more than I do, and you just got lucky."

"What happened?" Adam asked, his voice growing sincere.

He disliked all of this even more with Adam being sincere.

"She told me that she loved me. She demanded that I love her in return." His friends only stared at him. "I don't love her."

"Well, that's a bunch of bull—" Felipe said.

"You're an expert on love now?" Rafe cut in.

"More so than you," Felipe said. "Clearly."

"Love has never done a damn thing for me in my life. Specifically, loving Charlotte cost me my sight. It is a cosmic joke, or perhaps a message from the universe that my sight was restored after she left me."

"Or perhaps not. Perhaps it is simply a coincidence, and you are looking for any reason you can find to keep yourself from being happy." Felipe was simply standing there, regarding him far too closely with his enigmatic gaze.

"I do not want to keep myself from being happy," Rafe insisted. "That would be madness. Obviously, I would like some form of happiness in my life. If I didn't care about that, why would

I have gone to all this trouble to earn all of this damned money. To buy all of these damn things."

He picked a figurine up off his desk, one that reminded him of that best-beloved item his father had broken before throwing him out.

He hurled it against the wall.

"There, you see? And because I have money it means nothing to me. I can replace it. That is happiness."

"You are utterly full of rubbish," Felipe said. "You don't want to be happy. Because God forbid you feel anything good. Then it might be taken away from you."

"I like things I can control," Rafe said. "Do not tell me for one moment you aren't exactly the same."

"I was," Felipe said. "I was exactly the same as you, until I realized that a life you can control is empty."

"You think I don't understand?" Adam asked. "I have loved someone and lost them. I loved my first wife," he continued. "And she died. And falling in love with Belle was the most wretched, unwelcome thing that had ever happened since. I did not want to open up my heart. Not after everything I had lost. But I have. And it's worth it. It's worth it, because I have found the kind of happiness that I didn't know I could feel ever again. A kind of happiness I didn't know was possible."

"I'm not going to submit myself to certain loss," Rafe said, digging in. "Love costs too much. I've been there. I have done it. I have no desire to ever experience it again."

"And what about your children?" Adam asked. "Will you hold yourself back from them? What kind of father will you be? Will you be just like your own father?"

Rafe reached out, and he saw exactly where he could grab his friend by his jacket. Because he could see now. So really, Adam should be more careful. "Your face has already experienced damage, and I would hate to add to it," Rafe said. "But I will."

"I'm only saying," Adam said. "It seems to me that your father, your biological father, was emotionally stunted enough to kick out his mistress and his son. When you insulate yourself, you turn into a monster. Believe me—I know. I have been the monster in the castle, Rafe. Hiding away from the world. Shutting everyone out, doing terrible things. And love—Belle—that's how I found my way out. You are being offered salvation. A way out of the darkness. Maybe that's your metaphor."

Rafe took a step back, releasing his hold on Adam's jacket. "I will be there for my children. But this...is too much to ask."

"Because someday you might lose her?" Felipe asked.

"I lost her once," Rafe said, "and it quite literally nearly killed me."

"So you end things with her now? Before she could end them. Before something bad happened to her." Adam looked around the room; then he crossed to the desk and picked up a pointed letter opener. "I feel that perhaps you should go ahead and gouge your eyes out."

Felipe arched a brow. "I can't decide if I'm disgusted or truly impressed by this turn of events."

"I'm just saying. If you're going to try to prevent yourself from loss by causing the loss yourself, then you want to gouge out your own eyes. You have no guarantee you won't lose your sight again. Or perhaps, if that's too extreme, just tape them shut. While you have the ability to see, perhaps you should simply live the life of a blind man so that just in case something happens and this miracle is taken from you, you won't be disappointed."

The two men stared at each other, and Rafe said nothing.

Adam set the letter opener back down. "Or perhaps, my friend, for as long as you have sight, you should allow yourself to see."

"Damn," Felipe said.

"I'm ready to go," Adam said.

And with that, his scarred friend stormed out of the office.

Felipe lingered for a moment, regarding Rafe carefully.

"He has a point," Felipe said. "It pains me to admit it, but he does. He also had a point when I sent Briar away. About darkness and light, and the choices we all must make. The three of us have spent a fair amount of time standing in darkness, Rafe. Adam told me I had a choice to make. To continue to live in the shadows, or to walk into the light. You have that same choice now. You can have her. So you'd better damn well take her. If not, you aren't the man I believed you to be all this time. You are not the man I thought I knew." He reached out and touched the letter opener on Rafe's desk. "I know that you always felt unequal to us at school. Because we were royalty and you were from the gutter. But you were always a man whose stature exceeded that of nearly everyone around us. A man who had everything required of him to be a king. If you don't exhibit that now, then I am not sure if I ever really knew you."

And then it was Felipe's turn to walk out, leaving Rafe there with nothing more than a hollow ache in his chest.

Slowly he walked to the window and looked out at the view. At the sprawling vista of London below. Those iconic landmarks and the pink-and-orange sunset, slowly illuminating the waters of the Thames. Color. Light. He could see. And if it was taken from him again, it would surely be a deep, dark grief. To be reminded of the beauty that the world held only to lose it was unthinkable. But so was robbing himself of even a day without his sight now that it was back.

To gouge his eyes out now would be a foolish thing; there was no denying it.

To send Charlotte away when he had her love...

How was it any different? He was choosing to stand in the darkness when he could have the light. Was choosing to be isolated when he could have love.

But if he went after her, if he saw her, he would be lost to himself. There would be no controlling it. There would be no controlling his emotions, no regaining dominion over his heart. If he allowed himself to love her, then he was at the mercy of things that he could not control at all.

And so he had a choice. He could stand here with that semblance of pride, of being intact, and he could be alone. Or he could throw himself at her mercy and take the risk of being broken again.

The very idea was anathema to him. The idea of such a risk, the idea of such a loss.

But he thought of his life as it had been before when he'd had love. The warm house he had lived in, the time spent in Charlotte's arms. It was not the love that was lost. Love was the warmth. It was the color. It was the light.

Rafe had been given light again. But it was his choice as to whether or not he would remain in the darkness.

He was done with darkness.

He turned away from the window and strode out of his office.

CHAPTER FOURTEEN

CHARLOTTE WAS EXHAUSTED after a full shift. The shop was busy with people for the holidays, but she was enjoying working behind the food counters very much. She had never seen such a thing. All those lovely pastries stacked behind glass cases, like an edible rainbow that she wanted to eat in its entirety.

In fact, she had brought home a little box of cakes to enjoy for her dinner. Because she was sad, and she was pregnant, and if she could not have Rafe, then she would have cake. Because quite frankly a woman should have love and good sex or pastries.

Ideally a woman would have all three, she conceded as she flopped down onto the couch and opened up her box of cakes.

But she was not a woman in possession of all three. And so there would be cake.

She sighed, and lifted one of the treats to her lips, then froze when the buzzer for her door sounded. She stood up, sighing, and then getting spots of powdered sugar all over her black dress. She frowned, brushing at it uselessly, and then the buzzer sounded again.

She jumped and got even more powdered sugar on her. Giving up any semblance that she might remain somewhat unmussed, she popped the rest of the cake into her mouth, creating a small cloud of white that settled down onto the nice fabric.

She made her way over to the door and pressed the intercom. "Yes?"

"Charlotte," a very familiar, rich voice said. "It's me."

"What are you doing here?" she asked.

She had expected that he would come at some point. It wasn't as if she had thought she would never see him again. They were going to share custody of their babies; he would no doubt come to some of the doctor appointments. At least the ones with ultrasounds. So really, his presence was an inevitability that she was going to have to deal with. But she really didn't want to deal with it while she was covered in powdered sugar and exhausted from a work shift.

It did not appear that she had a choice.

"Why don't you come up?" She hit the button allowing him entry, then scurried into the bathroom to quickly brush her teeth.

It would not do for her to have bad breath when she saw him for the first time since he had cruelly stomped on her heart.

She scurried back out into the living area, then looked down and saw the white splashed across her black dress. She started to wipe the powdered sugar, then remembered he wouldn't be able to see her state, so she stopped messing with it.

There was a light knock at the door. "Come in," she called.

The door opened, and for the space of a breath, they just stood there with an expanse of floor between them, staring at each other.

"Rafe," she said finally, wishing that she hadn't

breathed his name out like she was a teenager meeting a rock star.

"Charlotte," he said. There was something different about his expression, something haunted, ravaged. He was staring at her, she realized. Really staring at her. As if…as if he could see her.

"Rafe?"

"Charlotte," he said her name again. "Charlotte." And then he was moving across the floor toward her, that expression going sharp and intense. He hauled her into his arms and he was kissing her before she could protest. Before she could do anything, say anything.

"Rafe," she said, repeating his name stupidly, because she didn't know what else to say.

"Charlotte. You…you're beautiful."

He looked haunted. And he looked nearly destroyed. Most important…he was looking.

"You can *see*?"

"I can. I…when you left me…I fell and I hit my head. The doctor thinks I reinjured myself in such a way that it has reversed some of the damage of my previous injury."

"That… Rafe…"

He took a deep breath, pushed his hand through his dark hair. "It happened a week ago. And it's why I have been avoiding you. Because I knew that if I saw you… Charlotte, now that I have seen you." He gripped her chin, holding her face steady. "Those blue eyes, just as I remember them. Hair…even more beautiful. The pink in your cheeks, the same as that color in your lips. Charlotte…I love you."

"What?"

"I love you. And I never stopped. Not in all these years. I could give any number of reasons for why I did not pursue a physical relationship with another woman. Not wanting to be with someone when I couldn't see. But most people make love in the dark, Charlotte, and frankly being with a woman as a blind man wouldn't have been such a terribly vulnerable thing. But I had excuses. And it was all because I couldn't imagine touching anyone that wasn't you. I couldn't imagine giving myself to somebody who wasn't you. I had found the one that my soul loved, and anything else would have been a farce. Would have been dishonoring what we had."

Her heart was hammering so hard she couldn't breathe. Her entire body was trembling, tears spilling from her eyes. It was a miracle that Rafe was here. A miracle that he was standing there with her. And that he could see. That he could see her. That was an even bigger miracle still.

"I never wanted anyone but you," she said. "I could never even consider it."

"I was so afraid to admit that I loved you. And I was…humbled by your bravery. Part of me felt like I didn't deserve it. Because you're right. In the face of all that you've been through your ability to love is nothing short of a miracle. But…we have miracles, Charlotte. I have a miracle. I can see you. God willing I'll be able to see our children. If this lasts. I have no guarantee that it will. It is somewhat unexplainable, and therefore there is no guarantee. Much like love. In life, we are given fragile, wonderful things. And…we may not get to keep them. But I would rather take a risk. I would rather have the happiest of days, however many there may be, than insulate my-self and stay in darkness and isolation. I want to stand in the light. I want to stand in it with you."

"I want that too," she said. "I want to be with you. And I don't know what else I want to do. With all of this newfound freedom that I have. But I know I want to love you. It is the one thing I have always known. Since I was eighteen years old and I was risking my life to do it. You were my first dream. And you're still my dream. Al-ways."

"I had forgotten about dreams. As a little boy I was shown that nothing in life was certain. And as a young man, I lost the only person that I cared for. You. I've lived in darkness ever since, and that has nothing to do with my vision. But you have taught me how to dream again, Charlotte. You have taught me how to love again. And this is not the first time you've taught me that. You taught me when I was twenty-five. You're teach-ing me again at thirty. I daresay you'll teach me again at forty. Sixty. Ninety. But it is my great joy to learn from you. For all the rest of my life."

"And it is my joy to teach you."

He pulled her into his arms, and he kissed her. And when he lifted his head, he looked deep into her eyes and he said, "Let down your hair."

EPILOGUE

CHARLOTTE WAS EXHAUSTED. The birth had not been an easy one. Hours of labor that had resulted in a C-section anyway, which Rafe had found to be a deep injustice and a test of his ability to remain calm.

Loving something put you at terrible risk. And watching his wife struggle as she had to bring their children into the world had certainly tested his sanity.

But now Charlotte was resting, and the babies were here.

A boy and a girl. The most perfect things Rafe had ever seen.

And he could see them.

He looked down at their pink, wrinkled faces, both babies cradled against his chest, one in each arm, and he felt his heart swell with pride and love. When he looked down at Charlotte, who was starting to drift to sleep, her pale golden lashes over her cheeks, her long golden hair loose around her shoulders, he thought his heart might burst altogether.

This was love. This was his family.

This was the truest and most real power in the world. It was not money. It was not status.

Rafe Costa had learned that the long and hard way. But thank God he had finally learned it.

"I have a present for you," Charlotte said, her tone sleepy.

"For me?" he asked. "That doesn't seem fair—you did all the work."

"Well, it's for you. And for the babies, as well. They're in my bag over there. If you open it up, you'll see them."

Frowning, he turned toward the far wall and went to retrieve her tote bag. In it were two small parcels, wrapped in plain paper.

"Unwrap them," she said.

He complied, slowly opening the paper, a flash of blue appearing as he tore the wrapping. It was a fish made of carnival glass. And in the other package was one identical to the first. Nearly identical to the one that had been destroyed by his father.

His chest constricted. It was almost impossible to breathe. "Charlotte..."

"We can't change the past, Rafe," she said softly. "But we can make our own future. No one can take this from us."

"I think these will be perfect in the nursery," he said, looking at the shimmering fish for a moment before placing them gently on the shelf nearest to him, already adorned with flowers sent by their friends.

"That's what I thought too." She looked down at the babies. "And hopefully they'll like them."

"If not, they can go in my office."

"Sounds good."

"Have you thought of what you want to name them?" he asked.

"The fish or the babies?" she asked.

"The babies," he responded, holding back a laugh.

Charlotte smiled, her full pink lips curving upward. "I did," she said sleepily.

"All right, what are your ideas?"

"Well, I was thinking that we ought to name them Adam and Philippa. You know, after your very good friends who suggested you either return to me or poke your own eyes out."

"Well, that is a suggestion," Rafe said, laughing.

But it was more than just a suggestion. His bride was quite adamant. So Adam and Philippa they were.

Which always created humor around the various gatherings over the years, as Adam and Belle and Felipe and Briar remained the best of friends with Rafe and Charlotte.

And whenever they were mentioned, it could truly be said that all of them lived happily ever after.

* * * * *

If you enjoyed
THE ITALIAN'S PREGNANT PRISONER,
why not explore the first two parts of
Maisey Yates's
ONCE UPON A SEDUCTION…
trilogy?

THE PRINCE'S CAPTIVE VIRGIN
THE PRINCE'S STOLEN VIRGIN

Available now!

SAME GREAT STORIES...
STYLISH NEW LOOK!

We're having a makeover!
From next month we'll still be bringing
you the very best romance from authors
you love, with a fabulous new look.

LOOK OUT FOR OUR STYLISH NEW LOGO, TOO

MILLS & BOON

LET'S TALK
Romance

For exclusive extracts, competitions
and special offers, find us online:

f facebook.com/millsandboon

◎ @millsandboonuk

🐦 @millsandboon

Or get in touch on 0844 844 1351*

For all the latest titles coming soon,
visit millsandboon.co.uk/nextmonth

Want even more
ROMANCE?

Join our bookclub today!